HAZEL
HILL
IS GONNA
WIN
THIS
ONE

HAZEL HILL IS GONNA WIN THIS ONE

MAGGIE HORNE

CLARION BOOKS

An Imprint of HarperCollins*Publishers*

Clarion Books is an imprint of HarperCollins Publishers.

Hazel Hill Is Gonna Win This One
Copyright © 2022 by Maggie Horne

ISBN 978-0-35-866470-3

22 23 24 25 26 PC/LSCC 10 9 8 7 6 5 4 3 2 1
First Edition

For Arthur, who is not a Tyler.

HAZEL HILL IS GONNA WIN THIS ONE

I've been told that it's impossible to know everything, but I think I've found a loophole.

Maybe I won't be able to know *everything*, but before I started middle school, I decided I could know *something*. I stayed up late making lists of all the subjects in which I might want to become an expert. Geometry. Giant pandas. Golf. And those were just the *G*s. I thought that by the time I got to high school, I'd know absolutely everything about one chosen subject, and maybe after that I could pick something else and go from there.

Not to brag, but we're only three months into seventh grade and I'm already the undisputed expert in one topic. And unfortunately, it's Tyler Harris.

I know which teachers he likes, and which ones like him. I know his birthday and his favorite color and his preferred candy bar. I know that, no matter how hard he tries, he always, *always* misspells the word *difficult* as *diffecult*. I know the name of every girl he's ever had a crush on, and, most importantly, I know when he has a secret.

I think the giant panda knowledge would have been much more useful, in the long term.

Today, it's raining, which means Miss A is running late and everyone's standing around talking at their desks. She's always late on rainy mornings because whenever there's a frog in the road she gets out of her car and moves it to safety.

That also means that today, Tyler is free to rush up to our desks.

"I have something to tell you," he says. "A secret. Do you want to hear it?"

At first, it was kind of fun to know all of Tyler's secrets. I thought maybe he'd give me something good, like information on a criminal syndicate or a ghost sighting. Then I realized that his secrets were always just that he had a crush on some girl, which would inevitably go away by the end of the week. There are only so many times a person can hear about Tyler Harris's feelings. And he has *a lot* of feelings. For a guy always so obsessed with making sure everyone knows he doesn't care about anyone else, he *always* has a crush on someone. I kept track, and so far he's told me about having crushes on twenty-seven different girls between last year and this year.

There are forty girls in our grade. Tyler Harris had a crush on 67.5 percent of them.

He's never asked me if I wanted to know a secret before. He's never really acknowledged that he tells me secrets, actually. There's a weird look in Tyler's eye today; kind of wild, kind of scary. His hair is sticking out in a million directions, like he's been up all night performing science experiments. Except I know Tyler barely ever does his homework, so that can't be it. His big eyes keep darting around the room, bouncing off my face to Miss A's empty desk to the dreary cream-colored classroom walls.

He looks angry, maybe. But I don't think it's at me.

"It's about Ella Quinn," he says.

I groan loud enough that a few people look over at us, and Tyler shushes me.

"I'm sure she's great," I say. "I'm sure she's perfect and you two are perfect and you're going to grow up and get married and have twenty-four perfect children and live in a mansion or whatever."

Ella Quinn and Tyler were the first couple to date when we got to middle school, if walking beside each other at recess counts as dating (in sixth grade, it definitely does). It clearly left a mark on both of them—they dated for a whole three months, and none of Tyler's other "relationships" have lasted as long. I know everything about Tyler Harris and I can barely keep up with those two; it seems like every other week Ella Quinn is holding his popcorn at the public skate again.

Tyler had been 100 percent onboard the Never Again Ella Quinn train until I caught him staring out the window for way too long during class and knew something was up. Like clockwork, the day before Thanksgiving break last week he told me he was going to ask her out again.

"It's not what you think," Tyler says, still way too intense. "Do you want to know or not? I could tell someone else instead. I could go and tell the whole school if I wanted to."

I lean back in my chair a little bit to avoid getting hit in the face with his spit.

"You're being weird. Are you okay?"

The second part slips out. Normally, I don't really care if Tyler is okay or not. It's just that this is the first time it's seemed like maybe he isn't.

Tyler rolls his eyes. "Do you even care what I have to say?"

The answer is no, but I don't think that's the answer Tyler wants to hear.

"Tell me, then," I say. "If it's such a big important secret that you have to tell me right away."

"Sit down, please, Tyler!" Miss A chirps, floating into the classroom. She's wearing a dress that has cats printed all over it and it looks like she hasn't brushed her hair in a week, and I'm so happy to see her. A grownup in a room changes the energy immediately: everyone calms down and goes quiet and everyone knows where they're supposed to look. Tyler can't keep talking to me. It's more of a relief than I expected.

"I hope you all had a wonderful Thanksgiving break," Miss A says. "And I *also* hope you've all begun to think about our annual speech competition."

I sit up as straight as I possibly can and wait for her to continue.

"I won the coin toss this year," she declares, "so I got to set your theme. I don't think anyone will be surprised to know that I've chosen history."

People around me groan, but I've known the theme since last week. Miss A likes me, and she appreciates a polite request.

"If that theme is too horrible for you, you're welcome to sit this one out," Miss A continues. "The speech contest is always for extra credit, and never mandatory. But! This year, I've decided that participation in the contest will exclude you from completing the final project in my history class. Whether you choose to compete in the speech competition alone or do the project with a partner, your assignments will be due the week before winter break. Those of you writing speeches, your work will be graded like an essay—it'll be excellent practice for high school."

I never realized that we were supposed to practice for high school. Then I got to middle school, and every time we did *anything* our teachers told us that it would be *great practice for high school* and we *won't be able to get away with that in high school*. But my cousin Amelia is in high school and she seems way more relaxed than me, so I'm still forming my opinions there. Then again, I guess Amelia isn't the "nightmares about being late for class" type.

People are looking at their friends from across the room, trying to figure out if they'd be better off doing the group project or the speech. I smile before I can stop myself. I get to win the speech competition *and* I don't have to do group work? Sometimes you just get handed a freebie.

"I'll give you guys some time to talk among yourselves and

work quietly on anything you need to get done this week," Miss A says. "You have just about three weeks to complete whatever it is you're planning on presenting, so you should have plenty of time to make some magic. As soon as the volume gets too loud, we'll be back to our friends the Pharaohs."

I grab my speech notebook out of my backpack before anyone's even out of their seats and smooth my hands over its beautiful red cover. There's nothing special about my notebook, really, but I know that the winning speech is tucked away inside here. It makes something kind of exciting and shimmery zing down my back when I see it.

I'm probably one of the only people working on a speech. My parents were surprised when I entered last year. I think they think that I don't have friends because I'm shy, but that's not it at all. I'm not shy, I'm just busy. My dad once told me he didn't have everything figured out yet, and he's at *least* thirty-five. If I'm going to figure out everything before then, I don't have time to do it with friends.

I've chosen a subject that's just cool enough for kids in my class to like, and just historical enough for Miss A to appreciate. "Unsolved Mysteries of the Twentieth Century." To be honest, I can't do any research at night because it freaks me out too much. But last year Ryden Stewart did his speech on *puberty* and he still gets laughed at, so I know I need to do something cool. Or at least just not something the judges call *certainly very . . . brave.*

I almost won last year. *Almost won* is my least favorite

phrase in the world. I'd been so sure of myself, one of the only sixth-graders competing against the rest of the school.

Then The Incident happened.

I thought it would be impressive for me to throw some big words in there — my parents always lose their minds when I whip out a word they didn't think I knew, like *efficacy* or *egregious* or *specificity*. My speech was about speeches, because I thought that would be funny (I still think it was kind of funny, but I'm probably the only one), and I wanted to say that some people use hyperbole, which is when you exaggerate a lot to make your point, in speeches.

Hyperbole is pronounced like *high-per-bull-ee*. I said *hyper-bowl*, and Ella Quinn, the *only* other sixth-grader competing against the whole school, won with her speech on the tooth fairy. The *tooth fairy*.

The memory makes me want to slam my head onto my desk, but I stop for two reasons:

1. I need my brain in top shape at all times.
2. Tyler has turned in his seat to face me and his creepy giant owl eyes are staring into my soul.

We look at each other and I try not to blink to show dominance, the way I read you have to do when you're training a puppy.

Ugh. Fine.

"What is it?" I ask. "Do you like a set of triplets now? Have you discovered the cure to the common cold? Are you and Ella Quinn adopting a cat together and moving to Siberia?"

Tyler's face goes weird again at the mention of Ella Quinn, and then he almost laughs.

Tyler and Ella Quinn's big breakup was the most dramatic scene to hit the Oakridge cafeteria in the last decade, probably. First semester was almost over and everyone was taking bets on whether they'd dance together at the winter dance. Three months of dating is like two and a half years in middle school time — Tyler had even given Ella Quinn a little silver necklace that had a charm shaped like a *T* on it. (I always wondered why on earth he thought that would be a good idea. Why would Ella Quinn want a dog tag around her neck? *If found, return to Tyler Harris.*) They broke up because a new girl moved onto Tyler's street and he wanted to, quote, *try his luck* with her. For the record, I know that that's ridiculous, but Tyler said that Ella Quinn was getting super possessive and demanding and rude to him anyway, and I have to assume no middle school relationship is worth that effort.

Ella Quinn ripped the necklace right off her neck and threw it so high that it got stuck on top of the big cafeteria clock. Apparently it's still there, but I'm too short to see it.

"Not quite," Tyler says. He looks like he's going to keep going, but Miss A walks by and he shuts his mouth.

"I'll stop listening in ten seconds," I say to Tyler after she's gone. "Starting now."

"Fine," he says. He looks around one more time to see if anyone might overhear us, and then pauses again.

I'm about to roll my eyes and get back to my speech—he can tell me whatever it is he wants to tell me later, if he's going to insist on making this so dramatic—but then he opens his mouth.

"Ella Quinn," he says, "has a *crush* on you."

2

All of the blood rushes out of my face.

I can do secrets about girls Tyler likes or girls who like Tyler. I can do complaints about his mom and brothers and teachers. I can nod along when he's droning on about hockey or shoes or whatever it is he loves. But I'm not sure I know how to respond to this.

"No, she doesn't," I say. I try to copy the face Tyler makes at me sometimes, like I'm so annoying he can't even believe he's talking to me. "Ella Quinn doesn't like girls."

Of course Ella Quinn doesn't like girls, but I've never actually met another girl who does, so maybe she does and I've just missed all the signs, but I'm pretty, *pretty*, almost a hundred percent sure that Ella Quinn doesn't like girls the way that I do. Let's call it 97 percent.

"She told me herself yesterday." Tyler shrugs. "She specifically said your name."

I try to drown out all the chattering and laughing and shrieking that comes with group work, try to ignore Tyler watching me carefully to see what I'm going to do with this information. It doesn't matter what Tyler's doing. It doesn't matter what *anyone's* doing. I need to *think*. I need to think, specifically, about three key points:

1. Could Tyler be telling the truth? I don't tend to take what he says very seriously, but also I don't really think he's ever lied to me before.
2. Is Ella Quinn *actually* gay?
3. Do I like Ella Quinn? Like, *like?*

I don't know the answers to the first two, but I'm almost positive the answer to number three is a big fat no. I'm sure Ella Quinn is fine as a person, but she's also technically my nemesis since she beat me in the speech contest. Also, if there's anything Tyler's told me in the last few months it's that Ella Quinn is a terrible girlfriend.

Not that I want Ella Quinn to be my girlfriend. If we're going off of what I want right now at this very moment, I'd be away from school, at home, in bed, eating something very cheese-heavy.

"Don't tell anyone," Tyler says, which is what he always says after one of his secrets.

It's different though, this time. He says it with a weird little smile, with this funny look in his eye like he's daring me to say something, like he wants me to run out and tell the whole school. I suddenly realize, very clearly, that when Tyler's friends call each other "gay," they mean "bad." Not that I didn't already know that, obviously—as if I'd be in the seventh grade and not notice that crappy kids call each other gay as an insult—but it's different to realize it like this, to see it in Tyler's eyes and know that he might actually believe it.

I don't think Tyler knows about me, but if you'd asked me last week if I cared if he did, I would have said no. Now I'm not so sure. Now I see that look.

He wants me to say something. He wants me to tell everyone in the school.

I don't know why, but sometime between their last breakup and now, Tyler decided he wants to ruin Ella Quinn.

"*You* aren't going to tell anyone, are you?"

"I don't know what you're talking about," he says, like we're sharing a joke but also like I *am* the joke. Tyler is really good at making people feel small in that weird way where you aren't sure if you're supposed to be upset or not.

"Don't bring me into it," I say. I know that sounds mean, but this is between Tyler and Ella Quinn. I don't think Tyler should try and out her, but I also *definitely* don't think Tyler should out *me*. This is the seventh grade. It's eat or be eaten.

"Why would I do that?" Tyler asks. He makes his eyes go big and innocent like when he's telling Miss A that he's just *bored* of doing work because what she's teaching isn't *challenging him enough*. I always roll my eyes when he does it to her, but now that it's directed at me, I can't quite tell if he's being serious or not.

I realize something then, though. Something that makes

my shoulders relax a little. I prop my elbow up on the desk and lean my head on my hand. I smile at Tyler and watch his face cloud over with confusion.

"You're right," I chirp. "You won't."

Tyler looks surprised that I sound so sure.

"Why wouldn't I?" he asks.

"Because you were going to ask Ella Quinn out again last weekend," I say. I'm remembering things as I speak, like when I'm in the heat of the moment during a speech contest and I can almost see every word I have to say laid out right in front of me without even trying. "Why would you tell *anyone* that she rejected you? What would people *think?* Maybe you wouldn't be able to tell people that she's a bad girlfriend if she doesn't want to get back together with you. Maybe they'd think that *you're* a bad boyfriend."

"Shut up," Tyler says. He says it quickly, hotly; his knuckles go white where they're gripping the side of my desk. "You don't even know what the hell you're talking about."

I might not, but I know enough to know that I've hit a nerve—and that I'm winning now.

"I know that I'm right," I say with a shrug. I feel much better now that I have the upper hand; Tyler doesn't seem nearly as menacing, and that's exactly how I like him. "You won't say anything, and I won't say anything, and we'll both just go on not saying anything."

Tyler looks like he's about to start saying some stuff a lot worse than *hell*, but Miss A walks by again.

"I guess we will, then," he says after a long pause.

"I guess we will," I agree.

But when Tyler goes back to his work and I go back to my speech, the two of us keep glancing at each other. Because I don't know what Tyler's plan is, or if he even has a plan in the first place. And he suddenly can't decide if he can trust sad little uncool Hazel with his secrets anymore.

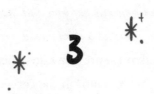

3

"So, the next time you see something you can't explain, think to yourself: Am I imagining things? Or are there some things in the world that are destined to remain a mystery? Thank you."

My mom stops the timer and she and my dad leap to their feet with applause. My dad even puts his fingers in his mouth and whistles, so you *know* they're being serious. I try to hide my smile.

"That was *wonderful*," my mom says. "And just over three minutes! I think if you slowed down a little more you'd clear that time limit for sure."

I nod, feeling a happy flush rise up on my face. I don't normally like practicing my speech in front of my parents, but I was driving myself bonkers reading it in front of the mirror in my room. Mirrors don't provide compliments *or* standing ovations.

"I think you did a great job of narrowing down the mysteries," my dad says. Doing that was his idea, so of course he's happy I did it.

"Thank you," I say, combing through a knot in my hair with my fingers. My mom's always offering to help me do my hair in the mornings, saying things like *you have the most gorgeous hair! It's so rich and dark and long!* but it's a slippery slope from braiding to *oh, you should just let me pick out your outfit today, honey! You don't need to wear the same jeans for a third day in a row!*

I'm about to ask if they're *sure* I don't need to add one more mystery when the baby monitor in the corner of the room starts making awful wailing noises and all three of us flinch at the exact same time.

My parents didn't expect to have Rowan—I'd made it eleven years as an only child, and they were always telling me that they were so happy with just me that they didn't need to have any other kids. Clearly, they weren't super tied to that idea. Now Rowan's been here for almost a year, and he's cute, but I can barely get through one round of speech rehearsals without him breaking up the party.

"I'm going to go check on him," my mom says, and then makes very intense eye contact with me. "I'm going to come right back down here, and we can talk about your speech for as long as you want. And then maybe we can have some ice cream?"

I've been eating a lot of ice cream the last year or so. When my mom found out she was going to have Rowan, she read a bunch of books about introducing a new baby to an only child and most of them told her to make sure I didn't feel left out or neglected. They made me go to a Big Sister class at the hospital and I was the oldest one there by a *lot*. They showed us how to put a diaper on a baby doll and I *clearly* did it better than any of the toddlers, but I still haven't been allowed to change a diaper. Why have a second baby when your other kid is eleven and not even let her help? Ridiculous.

I guess my mom's version of making sure I don't feel left out or neglected is always offering me ice cream. At the rate we're going, my adult teeth are going to fall out before my brother grows his baby teeth.

Mom leaves the room to hurry upstairs, but not before she gives my dad a Significant Look. That usually means I'm about to be forced to have a conversation about my feelings.

"Do you actually want ice cream?" Dad asks once Mom's out of the room.

"I always want ice cream. I'm twelve."

He nods like I said something very important and serious.

"So!" he says, stretching out on the couch and poking me with his gross sock foot until I hop out of the way. "Seventh grade!"

"Seventh grade!" I repeat. I try to make my voice go deep like his and he laughs.

"How's it treating you so far?" he asks. "How are the other kids? Anyone new? Anyone exciting? How's that Tyler boy you always talk about?"

I do *not* always talk about Tyler. Sometimes I have to complain about him, and since I don't have a best friend to do that with, the duty falls to my parents. They can have a straight-A student who *occasionally* has to talk about the obstacles in her life, or they can have a slacker who has a lot of friends and screechy sleepovers that keep them awake all night. So far, I haven't heard either of them ask for the second option.

I talk about way more stuff than just Tyler Harris, is what I'm getting at.

"Consistently irritating," I say.

"Well, sometimes there's merit in that!" Dad chirps. "I'm pretty sure I annoyed your mother into marrying me."

"That doesn't sound very romantic."

Dad considers that for a second, but I think he knows I'm right. I know what he's implying: that I have some kind of crush on Tyler and it's very cute. Normally that's frustrating—I don't have some kind of crush on *anyone*, but I especially won't have one on a boy anytime soon, or ever—but today it just freaks me out a bit. My plan has always been that I'd tell my parents about my no-boys-allowed policy if there was something to report. If I actually liked Ella Quinn, maybe I'd say something now, but I don't, so I won't. First of all, I'm still, like, 92 percent sure that Tyler was lying. Second, thinking about all of this just leaves a bad feeling in my stomach. I did everything I could to ignore Ella Quinn for the rest of the day today, but tomorrow my schedule changes and we have science together after homeroom. I think I'd rather dissect something than deal with that.

"You don't have to worry about me, you know," I tell my dad. I know that when he looks at me like that, like he's trying to figure me out, that he's concerned about how I'm doing. He and my mom spend so much time worrying about whether I'll turn out okay that sometimes I can't tell if they think I'm okay right now.

"I'm fine," I say, because I know that's what my dad's asking.

"You know you can invite anyone you want over here, right?"

"I know."

The unspoken *so why don't you?* hangs in the air, but Dad doesn't actually say it. It's just that, as Tyler Harris's personal secret keeper, I know how messy friends can be. Someone is always mad at someone, or hiding something from someone, or pretending not to care when they do. It's too much to keep up with—and those are just the boys! All I've seen from the girls is more secrets, more hiding, more pretending, more anger. I mean, Tyler told me that Ella Quinn told him he wasn't a very good kisser *right after* their first date!

Not that I'm planning on kissing Ella Quinn. But *still*.

"I'm fine," I say. "Really. I like keeping to myself. I like being able to do whatever I want without worrying about hurting anyone's feelings. I like my spot. I don't have anything in common with any of the girls in my grade."

"Oh, I'm sure that's not true!" my dad says.

"They only care about boys in our grade and boys in bands and boys who play sports and boys they like and boys who like them. And the *boys* only care about girls in our grade and girls in bands and girls who play sports and girls they like and girls who like them. You can't hold a conversation with any of them."

Okay, so I don't *actually* know if that's true. Of course I've had conversations with girls in my grade before. In elementary school I had friends. I went to birthday parties and had inside jokes and gave hugs. But then those friends turned out to live in a different middle school district and they haven't bothered to try and track me down since I started at Oakridge. And now everyone is only interested in talking about boys and Tyler's only interested in talking about how girls are only interested in talking about boys, but at least he's so self-centered he doesn't even think about who *I* might like.

My dad gives me a look that makes me squirm. Like he's about to start talking to me about how *one day, you might want to talk about boys, too.*

Thankfully, that's the exact moment my mom comes downstairs with a very awake, *very* cranky Rowan.

He gets me ice cream *and* out of awkward situations—I don't know why my mom was so worried about me liking my brother.

4

Ella Quinn's name isn't really Ella Quinn.

I mean, it is, but it's her full name. First name Ella, last name Quinn. Everyone calls her by her full name, and I still don't really understand why, especially since we have, like, fifteen girls named Bella at Oakridge and only one Ella.

Ella Quinn isn't in my homeroom—she has Mr. Pitts, who I had nightmares about before school started because last year he threw a chair at a wall, and as much as I'm afraid of that, I'm even more afraid of what my parents would do if they knew I was being taught by a guy who throws chairs at walls. The amount of emails my dad would write *alone* makes me shudder.

My schedule rotates today, so I have science in the morning. That means I'll be face-to-face with Ella Quinn right away. I considered faking sick to get out of it, but Rowan is going through what my mom calls *a sleep blip,* which is her polite way of saying *my kid won't shut up at night.* She ended up oversleeping when he finally did fall asleep, and we had to rush out the door. No time for me to even think about what kind of sick I'd pretend to be.

Ella Quinn sits in the row ahead of me, so I can't tell if she's looking at me differently when I get into class. I don't know if anything's weird because the *weirdest* thing would be Ella Quinn going out of her way to talk to me in the first place.

Ella Quinn isn't mean. This isn't one of those things where I'm the poor, sad, lonely girl who doesn't have any friends and Ella Quinn is the popular, pretty, smart girl whose friends all hate me and don't let me sit with them, or whatever. She's my nemesis, for sure, but she's never been mean to me.

I don't actually know if I'm *her* nemesis, which could explain that.

The bell hasn't rung yet, so I have time to stare at the back of Ella Quinn's head. She's sitting beside her best friend, Riley, and I still don't know how they made that happen because our science class has assigned seating. Their heads are very close together, considering we had three head lice outbreaks last year, and they're whispering furiously at each other. Every so often one of them writes something carefully on a piece of paper and the other looks at it, shakes her head or nods, and then rips the paper up into tiny pieces.

It's like they're *spies*. When I started middle school and everyone was acting differently, it was suddenly like I didn't speak the same language as everyone else. I don't think Ella Quinn and Riley's language is even from the same planet as mine.

I keep watching them as if they're going to just turn around and say, *Hazel, would you like to understand exactly what we're talking about and why?* Ella Quinn keeps taking off her gold wire glasses and polishing them on her shirt. Every time she takes them off, more of her blond hair escapes from its French braid and it somehow makes it look even better, like she's famous. Eventually, she puts one of her arms around Riley and squeezes, and Riley kind of deflates, her low brown ponytail slipping off her shoulder and hanging sadly down her back. Ella Quinn puts her (hopefully lice-free) head on top of Riley's and they stay like that for a while.

I squint at them. Not to be bigheaded or anything, but that definitely seems like the behavior of people with a secret.

They separate, turning to face each other so I can see both their profiles. Ella Quinn leans back and makes a weird face at Riley. At first, she doesn't seem too impressed, but Ella Quinn keeps at it and Riley laughs, covering her face with her hands.

There's a twinge in my stomach that I try to push down. I'm not a monster. Of course I notice that people seem to be really happy with their friends. But it also seems like the people who are friends just *fit* together in a way that I don't think I fit anyone else. Everything I've seen and everything Tyler's ever told me has more than proven that. Sometimes I think that maybe everything'll change again when I'm finally in high school and I'll fit someone there, but maybe it won't. Maybe this is just the kind of person I am.

I shake my head to forget all of that. That's not the point. The *point* is that I'm sitting on possibly the biggest secret to ever hit our grade, and I have no idea what I'm supposed to do with it.

I almost weep with relief when Mrs. Haig finally walks in. She's the type of teacher to cut right to the chase, and she doesn't disappoint. Suddenly the only thing I'm supposed to think about is the water cycle, and I can do that. I can shut my brain off to everything except science.

I almost believe myself when I think that.

I don't stop thinking about it. I *try* to stop thinking about it, but no matter what I try to think about—the rules of poker, the surviving members of the Beatles, the lost city of Atlantis, the names of all the Teletubbies, my pet hamster who died three years ago (rest in peace, Mozzarella)—my head keeps coming right back to Ella Quinn and Riley. I don't know why they would sit and talk like that if they didn't have a secret. I don't know why Ella Quinn would say my name specifically. I don't *know*, and it's becoming extremely annoying.

It's just.

It's just.

It's just that I don't know. If Ella Quinn *did* say what Tyler said she said, did she say it because she really meant it? Or did she say it because she sees me as an easy target? Someone who she can just throw under the bus without even thinking about it? Did she say it because she thought it would be funny, for some reason? Is she as catty as Tyler always used to say that she was?

But if she *did* mean it, I wonder if she would want to talk about it. I wonder if she ever wonders what it would be like to talk about this kind of thing with someone who gets it, the way I do. I wonder if she saw something in me and recognized it. I wonder if she feels like me, sometimes, if she thinks about her whole life stretching out long and dark and foggy in front of her and if she's as terrified as I am by how much she doesn't know about what it will look like.

I wonder if she, maybe, possibly, needs someone to talk to right now.

I'm still thinking that by the end of the day, once the bell rings and everyone starts screaming and running around. It's like they've been trapped in this school for ten years and *not* like it's a Tuesday so we'll be right back here tomorrow morning. I'm still thinking about it when we all have to pretend like we're lining up for the bus, but really everyone is just gathered outside in a big clump. I stand a little farther back and when a bus monitor walks by, everyone tries to act like we've been in line the whole time. I shudder into the winter coat my mom made me wear this morning because *it'll feel like winter out there today, Hazel.* I told her I wouldn't need it, but I guess I should trust the one of us who actually watches the Weather Channel. It does, in fact, feel like winter.

Ella Quinn is on my bus. I've never given it too much thought because we're both on the Out There bus—the one for kids who live in big farmhouses outside of town (Ella Quinn) or in the rickety old post office building off the town's main street (me), instead of the tidy subdivisions everyone else is getting bused to. We have the longest route. It winds through forests and back roads and through farms and empty fields, but there are only about twenty kids on my bus, which means I never have to worry about having to sit beside anyone.

Not that Ella Quinn would sit beside me, anyway—Riley

and her mom live in a log cabin in the middle of the woods, so she's on our bus too and Ella Quinn and Riley sit beside each other. That's just the rule. Today, they're talking to each other the way they were in science; close together, quiet, like no one else is even around. Riley's animated, waving her arms around and pointing in a bunch of different directions. One of her points is in *my* direction, and I look away quickly. Tyler's on one of the other buses, so he could be anywhere. If he saw me staring at them, he'd probably start to wonder why I was so interested in the whole situation, and that could only end badly.

Except then Ella Quinn breaks away from Riley, walks over to me, and quietly asks, "Do you mind if I sit with you today?"

5

The first thing I do is look over at Riley, but she's not looking at me. In fact, she's not looking at anyone. She's looking up at the sky, doing an impression of Tyler's innocent face.

"Why do you want to sit with me?" I ask, and then feel immediately bad when Ella Quinn's face falls. "I mean, don't you want to sit with Riley?"

"Not today!" Ella Quinn says. I don't know how to say no without sounding rude. So when the bus rolls up, we both let Riley get on and sit in the front seat. Ella Quinn leads the way farther back, past my usual spot on the tire, which I look at longingly as I walk by.

We sit beside each other, but for a while we don't say anything. Other people crowd onto the bus and give us weird looks, but Ella Quinn is friends with a few of the eighth-graders and none of them ask any questions. I'm in the window seat, which I appreciate, because it means I can stare outside and pretend like I'm alone on the bus. Of course, Ella Quinn doesn't let that last for very long.

"Are you going to skate tonight?"

I don't want to be *completely* rude, so I try to hide the face I make at the question. Of course I'm not going to the public skate tonight. Everyone makes such a big deal out of it. It's every Tuesday down at the old arena and you pay three dollars (five dollars if you want a hot chocolate too) and everyone skates in circles or else just stands around and gossips. I went exactly once, with my dad, the first week of middle school before I realized friends weren't in my future at Oakridge. Everyone ignored me because they already had their friend groups. Why would you make space for someone new if you didn't have to? Public skate isn't school, where teachers throw kids without partners into groups. It's the closest thing we've got to the Real World so far.

"No," I say, instead of saying any of that.

Ella Quinn nods slowly, just sort of bobbing her head. Both of us look like we'd rather be sitting somewhere else.

"You should go sometime," she says. "I know it might not be your thing, but it can still be fun. You could hang out with me and Riley if you wanted."

I feel about a million things at once. What is she trying to *do?* If any part of me is interested in making friends, it starts to light up at Ella Quinn's invitation. But a bigger part of me starts to think in overdrive. What are the odds that Ella Quinn chooses *today* to talk to me, the day after Tyler tells me that big secret?

"Maybe some other time," I say.

I have zero intention of *ever* going to the public skate.

Ella Quinn and I sit in silence for a while. Normally I don't mind the bus ride, but today the stopping and starting makes me feel nauseous. I lean my head against the window and watch the fields zip by. If I unfocus my eyes I can almost pretend like Ella Quinn isn't sitting beside me.

"Hey Hazel?" she asks. So there goes that plan.

"Yeah?"

Ella Quinn chews on her bottom lip. "How often do you talk to Tyler?"

I stiffen. "Why would he talk to me? Do you really think Tyler cares enough about me to talk to me about anything?"

"That doesn't answer the question."

I think about how I should answer for a long minute.

"I talk to him sometimes," I say.

In theory, I guess I should be on Team Ella Quinn here. I think if you add up all the nemesis points and stack them up against the feminist points and the Tyler-kind-of-sucks-sometimes points, things *just* about come out in favor of Ella Quinn. But also, this is one of the only times she's ever spoken to me, and even though he probably wouldn't admit to it and neither would I, Tyler talks to me all the time. I don't know if I should be protecting his secrets or listening to Ella Quinn's or what.

"What are you doing your speech on this year?" I ask her to try to change the subject.

It sort of works. Ella Quinn sits up straighter.

"Maybe I'll tell you, if you actually answer my question first."

Ugh.

"We talk when there's something to talk about," I say. "We

have the same homeroom, so sometimes we have to talk about homework or whatever."

Ella Quinn thinks that over for a while as the bus drops off Brenna Park, one of her billion friends. Brenna stops for a second and squeezes Ella Quinn gently around the shoulders before she goes on her way.

"Does she know she'll see you again tomorrow?" I ask once Brenna's off the bus and we're moving again.

Ella Quinn scrunches her face up. "You don't think it's nice to care about your friends?"

I don't really know what to say to that that won't make me sound like a monster. So I don't say anything at all.

Maybe this wouldn't be so bad if I knew I was about to get off the bus, but Ella Quinn must have planned this. I'm the very last stop. The bus twists through the woods and the farms and drops everyone off before we go back into town because my house is near the bus depot. I ride alone in silence with Krystal the Bus Driver for the last ten minutes of the trip and honestly sometimes it's the best part of my day. Ella Quinn's stop is somewhere in the middle. For the first time, I think I'd like to switch places with her life.

"Poison," Ella Quinn says after another stretch of silence.

"What?"

"That's what I'm doing my speech on," she continues, picking at a hole in the gray vinyl bus seat. "Poison. Different types, famous poisoners, that kind of thing."

From the tooth fairy to *poison?* I had thought Ella Quinn

was going to talk about, like, the Easter Bunny, and my super-cool unsolved mysteries speech would win no problem, but *poison* is something else entirely. She's playing to win just as much as I am.

I spend a minute thinking about all of the improvements I'll have to make to my speech to be more competitive. I should definitely add that other mystery now, and maybe I should go through and make sure the ones I'm talking about are as cool as they possibly can be, but then I stop.

I know how much I want to win the speech contest, but I *also* know how much Ella Quinn wants to win it, too. Before now, I wouldn't dream of telling her my topic, but she asked to sit with me on the bus and she told me her topic when I asked. Even if she *is* the super annoying girlfriend Tyler always says she is, she's at least trying to be nice to me.

Here's what happens: I mean to turn to Ella Quinn and tell her my topic. I was going to tell her, and then maybe she would feel like we're on a level playing field, and we could talk about our speeches and why no one else in our classes seems to care about the contest when I know we both do. I could almost have an okay bus ride home sitting beside her.

Instead, without thinking, I say, "Tyler told me what you told him."

Ella Quinn's whole body zaps up like she was struck by lightning. Her face goes pale and I swear her braid jumps up in the air like a spooked cat. (Though we might have just gone over a bump in the road.)

At first, it seems like she doesn't know how to respond. She looks around us as if everyone's going to be listening in on our conversation, but then realizes that's ridiculous.

"If you want to talk about it, you can," I say. "I . . ."

I don't get to finish my sentence because the bus has stopped again. This time, it's Riley who appears at our seat.

"Oh!" Ella Quinn says, looking up at Riley like she's forgotten who she is. "Are we already here?"

"Yes ma'am," Riley says. She doesn't make eye contact with me, but smiles in my general direction.

"I'm going to Riley's tonight so her mom can take us skating," Ella Quinn explains to me.

I nod. "Cool. Well, see you—"

"Hazel," Ella Quinn says. Riley's gone up ahead to tell Krystal that Ella Quinn will be *right there* (if there's one thing Krystal doesn't like, it's stragglers). "Will you come to public skate tonight? I really, really think you should."

"I mean, I don't usually go," I say. Ella Quinn is starting to look like Tyler did earlier, all intense and frazzled like my parents the first few weeks of Rowan's life.

"I need to talk to you," she says. "It's important. It's probably better to talk about it outside of school."

I don't know why it happens, but something in me loosens toward Ella Quinn just then. Maybe it's because she looks so freaked out, or because she's *begging* me to come skating even though I never go and no one's ever asked me to before. Maybe it's because Tuesdays are my least favorite day of the week and I've been weakened by this one.

But whatever the reason, I say, "Yeah, okay," and Ella Quinn lets out all the air in her lungs and says, "Thank you."

Ella Quinn gets off the bus, and I drop my face into my hands.

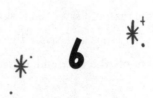

6

I think my mom almost has a heart attack when I mention public skate at dinner.

"You want to go?" she asks.

It's honestly a little offensive. Okay, fine, I haven't been the most social person in the world the last year or so. But is it really such a shock to think I might go to a social occasion with people from school?

(I recognize that I just thought I had zero intention of ever going to public skate, but my mom doesn't need to know that.)

"Yeah," I say. "A girl in Mr. Pitts's class invited me on the bus."

"You want to go," my mom repeats. "We aren't forcing you to go? You just *want* to go?"

"Well, not if you don't stop treating me like I'm a freak for it!"

My parents lose it at the exact same time at that. They both start talking over each other saying things like *of course you aren't a freak!* And *we're just excited for you!* and *you just let us know when you want to leave!* And *we can go right now if you want, let me grab my purse.*

"I don't need you guys to come with me," I say quickly. "I mean, no offense. But parents don't really go to this."

"So that arena just lets a bunch of twelve-year-olds go wild every Tuesday night?" my dad asks.

I sigh. "Okay, *some* parents go. But Riley's mom is taking Ella Quinn, so we're covered in terms of parents."

"Who's Riley?" my mom asks.

"Ella Quinn's friend," I say.

"Who's Ella Quinn?" my dad asks.

"We don't have *time* for this!"

In the end, my dad convinces my mom to let me go alone. There are a lot of serious looks that I think mean *we can't stunt our daughter's growth* and *this is a very delicate age* and *socialization is crucial.*

My parents read a lot of books about how to be the world's best parent. I don't think there's, like, a competition they can enter, but they *definitely* would if they could.

I think about changing out of my hoodie and jeans before we leave for the arena, but then I decide that's silly. I'm not putting forward any extra effort because, the way I see it, there are only two possible outcomes:

1. I could be walking into a trap, where Ella Quinn is organizing everyone to laugh at me and make fun of me

for being gay and I'll freak out and then I won't have any friends until *college.*

2. Ella Quinn is about to come out to me, which would be very strange since we've barely ever even spoken before and I'd have no idea what to do with that information. But I thought about what I'd like when I ever decide to tell someone about me, and I think I'd find it really weird if they dressed up for the occasion.

It isn't until my dad is parking the car that I realize I don't actually know for sure if Ella Quinn and Riley are *going.* Sure, Ella Quinn said she was, but why am I supposed to believe anything she says? If you ask Tyler, nothing she says can be trusted. I'm sure she's not *that* bad, but I have nothing else to go off of.

"You have to promise you'll come get me the *second* I call you," I say to my dad, sinking into my seat. "The *millisecond.*"

It gets dark so early now that it's almost December, and the sun has already set behind the trees outside of the rink. I recognize nearly everyone walking inside, lit up by the arena's glow and always in pairs or groups. They all look much more comfortable than I feel.

My dad picks up his phone and types our home address into his maps app. Once he punches everything in, the screen says it takes five minutes to get between here and home.

"I can't promise milliseconds," he says. "But I'll be here in five minutes. Four if I don't hit the light. Think of me like a pizza delivery guy: under five minutes or it's free."

"It's free either way," I say. "You're my dad."

But I'm smiling, which means my dad knows he's done a good job, so he looks very proud of himself when he drives away. He's probably going to go home to my mom and tell her all about his Parenting Win. (That's the name of one of the books they've read, by the way.)

"It's a big block of ice," I mutter to myself once my dad's gone and I'm alone in the parking lot. "It's just a room full of ice."

And everyone you know, a helpful voice in my head reminds me. The big brown building looks menacing. Not the same place kids used to have birthday parties when we were little. Now it's somewhere *things happen* and *people talk.*

"Hazel!"

I've never in my *life* been happier to see Ella Quinn.

"Oh, hi," I say. I hope it doesn't sound too relieved. What I actually want to say is *oh my god you're actually here thank god I thought I was going to have to go inside by myself and I can't even skate why the heck am I even here?!*

"Thanks for coming," she says. Her hair's down now, but she's wearing a beanie in that way cool girls can pull off but I never can. "I know this isn't usually really your thing."

It's true that I never go to the public skate, but I still bristle. I don't like it when people assume things about me.

"What was the big thing you wanted to talk to me about?" I ask.

Ella Quinn squirms, just enough for me to notice. "Riley's just saying bye to her mom," she says instead of answering me. "I said we'd meet her in the lobby. Wanna go in and then we can talk?"

I shrug, because I don't know how this is actually supposed to work. Ella Quinn takes that as a yes and leads the way inside.

There's a guy at the counter when we get inside stamping everyone's hands. He looks too tall for his body, like he got stretched out overnight. He seems just about as excited as I am to be here. Ella Quinn makes a noise that kind of sounds like *damn it* beside me, but I ignore her.

The guy perks up when he sees Ella Quinn, sitting up straighter and giving both of us a big smile.

"Is this your little sister?" he asks Ella Quinn, and it takes me a second to realize he's talking about me.

I don't look super young, okay? I think I look exactly the way a twelve-year-old is supposed to look. I'd describe everything about me as *medium*. I think twelve is a medium age! I think it works out!

But Ella Quinn is . . .

Ella Quinn has . . .

The thing with Ella Quinn is that . . .

Look. There isn't a polite way to say this. Ella Quinn has boobs. Ella Quinn has the kind of boobs that we aren't supposed to even think about having for another two years at least. The kind of boobs people talk about super uncomfortably.

The kind of boobs that, I guess, make the high school guy taking tickets stare at her.

Well, stare at *them*.

"She's my friend," Ella Quinn says to the guy. I jolt a little. I was expecting her to say *ew, no, of course she's not my sister.* "We're both in the same class at school. *Middle school.*"

The guy's eyes snap back up to Ella Quinn's face, but he doesn't seem to feel as guilty as I think he should. He stamps our hands and Ella Quinn snaps hers away from him quickly so their fingers don't touch.

"Does that . . ." I start, and Ella Quinn finishes the thought for me before I can finish.

"Literally all the time," she says. "And I'm not using *literally* wrong there, either. *Literally* all. The. Time."

She rolls her eyes like it doesn't bother her, but her face is bright red and she rushes ahead even though she said we'd wait for Riley in the lobby. I hurry along behind her and get embarrassed when we pass some classmates. They probably think I'm following Ella Quinn around and she's trying to avoid me.

"Do you skate?" Ella Quinn asks me once she decides we're far enough away from the lobby. "Sorry, I guess I should have asked you that before I said you should come here."

Everyone in our town skates. That's why it's so embarrassing that I don't.

But Ella Quinn isn't asking the way other people have asked me, where it's more like *why can't you skate, you freak?* It doesn't sound like she'd care either way.

I remember a conversation I had with Tyler last month. He said that he was talking to Ella Quinn, and he made a joke with her that she laughed at, but then she told her mom and her mom thought it was inappropriate and Tyler got in trouble with Ella Quinn's mom. It reminds me that I shouldn't trust things about Ella Quinn just because she seems harmless.

"It doesn't matter," I say. I try to flip my hair but I think it comes across more like a muscle spasm. "I didn't come to skate. You said you had something you needed to talk to me about."

There's that squirm again. I'm about to square my shoulders and demand that Ella Quinn just explain what's going on, but before I can even open my mouth she's smiling because Riley finally found us.

"We can talk about that later!" Ella Quinn says. "Do you want popcorn? My treat!"

It's just really hard to say no to popcorn.

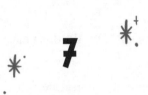

7

Riley and I do that thing where we acknowledge each other like we've hung out before. It would be weirder to introduce ourselves to each other. It's not like we've never met, but it's also not like we've ever actually done anything together, either.

I've never really given much thought to Riley. She's always just been Ella Quinn's best friend and that's that. Sometimes I see them talking to the other popular girls, but the two of them are always together. A unit.

If Ella Quinn was going to have a crush on a girl, I find it hard to believe that it would be on me and not Riley.

"So Hazel doesn't skate—"

"I never said I didn't skate," I say, cutting Ella Quinn off, and then immediately regret it. I should probably get better about letting people assume things about me *sometimes*. Especially when they're right.

"Oh!" Ella Quinn says. "Sorry. Do you want to skate, then? I only said that because Riley and I don't usually skate."

"I can't skate," Riley says, and then I feel stupid for feeling stupid.

Rats.

I try to play it cool. "Oh. We don't have to skate, then. That's fine."

Ella Quinn politely ignores the fact that I don't even have any skates with me, which probably would have made skating a little bit more difficult.

We make our way over to the concession stand and my mouth starts to water right away. There's just something about fake butter smell that makes me feel like I could eat the biggest size popcorn they have plus a slice of pizza plus a bag of candy.

I mentally add *why popcorn is so good* to my list of possible speech topics for next year.

"Riley," Ella Quinn says before we get in line. "If I gave you my money, would you order for us?"

Ella Quinn is looking over our heads at the concession stand. There's another teenage boy working behind the counter. At least, I'm pretty sure he's different from the one who stamped our hands. Boys all tend to blur together.

Riley takes the money from Ella Quinn and heads over to the line. At first, I assume I should stay with Ella Quinn, since she's the one who invited me and I've never really spoken to Riley before. But then Ella Quinn says, "Seriously, Hazel, grab anything you want. I babysat last weekend so I'm flush with cash," and I think that means she wants me to go wait in line with Riley.

I shuffle over awkwardly, but Riley makes room for me once I get up to where she's standing.

"So is every guy in here so obsessed with Ella Quinn that she can't get her own popcorn?" I ask.

It's not my best moment. The thing is, I'm honestly more used to talking to Tyler than I am to talking to girls. With Tyler, it's usually a pretty safe bet that saying something like that about Ella Quinn would get you a great response. He'd laugh and then tell me more of his secrets and, honestly, it's nice to feel useful like that sometimes.

I've kind of forgotten that in Girl World, people are actually friends. Of course Riley wouldn't react the way Tyler would to me saying something negative about Ella Quinn. I know that Tyler says Ella Quinn doesn't care about anyone but herself, but I'm realizing there's no way that's true. Even if she doesn't care about *me*, she definitely cares about Riley. And Riley cares about her.

I bet Ella Quinn and Riley hate people assuming things about them, too.

"She almost had a panic attack before we got here," Riley says to me, looking me up and down like she's trying to see if she could fight me. "She wouldn't exaggerate how guys treat her and how it makes her feel."

I immediately feel like crap.

"Sorry," I mutter, but Riley doesn't respond.

When we finally get to the front of the line, Riley orders three popcorns and then, after a pause, picks up a bag of sour candy. Before she can put it on the counter I dig in my pocket and pull out enough change to pay for it.

"Really," I say once we've gotten our stuff. "Sorry. That was gross of me to say."

Riley smiles and offers me one of the red candies from the bag. That's obviously the best color, so I think she actually forgives me.

Once we're in the arena, snacks in hand, I follow Riley and Ella Quinn to what's clearly their usual seat in the stands. It's the perfect spot to watch everyone skate—close enough to see who's who, but far enough away to talk about them without them hearing you.

Before we even sit down, one of the girls from Mr. Pitts's class whose name I can't remember rushes up to us and starts talking to Riley about the project they're doing together. In my head, there are two types of people: people who are doing the speech contest and people who aren't. I guess Riley is a person who isn't.

The girl drags Riley away, and then I remember why I'm actually here. I think Ella Quinn remembers it at the same time as me, because she starts looking around to make sure no one can hear us and sinking into her seat.

Before I know it, I feel bad for her. I feel *bad* for Ella Quinn. Even if she isn't hiding this big huge secret, she's clearly hiding *something*. She *told me her speech topic*.

"Hazel—"

"Me too."

We talk over each other and then laugh awkwardly.

"Sorry," Ella Quinn says. "What did you say?"

I take a very deep breath. "Tyler told me what you said to him yesterday. About . . . about liking . . . girls?"

I don't want to say anything about her liking *me*, because what if that was all a lie and Tyler just wanted to mess with both of us? I know that I'm great, but I still find it very hard to believe that someone out there would have a crush on me, let alone a girl, and nothing seems worse than thinking someone *does* like me only to find out that it was all a lie, or a joke.

"Oh my god," Ella Quinn says. She brings both her hands up to her face. "Oh my god, Hazel, I'm so sorry."

All the blood drains from my face so quickly that I get dizzy. My head is spinning. Everyone in this arena could be sitting in front of us right now, watching the show, and I wouldn't even notice.

"So, what, you just thought it would be funny to say you were gay?" I ask. It feels easier to be mad right now than anything else. "Because that's so hilarious, right? Because no one's *actually* gay, right?"

"No!" Ella Quinn has tears in her eyes and that makes me even angrier. She doesn't get to be sad! I'm the one who should be crying, and I'm pretty sure I'll start once I get home.

Home. I pull out my phone and text my dad, *come get me. 5 mins.*

"I'm so sorry," Ella Quinn says. "I never thought he would tell you what I said, I just . . . I needed him to stop."

"To stop what?" I roll my eyes. Of course Ella Quinn didn't think about whether or not it would affect me to go and tell Tyler Harris that she had a crush on me. Of course she didn't think about anyone but herself.

"I . . ." Ella Quinn trails off. "Can you keep a secret?"

A laugh bursts out of me. Is this what being hysterical feels like?

"Yeah, I'm pretty good at secrets."

"Tyler is . . ." Her face is bright red and she leans in closer, ducking her head so that I have to do the same. "He won't leave me alone. At first I thought he wanted to get back together because he missed me, but then he started saying all of these things that made me super uncomfortable and I told him I didn't think it was a good idea. That was over the summer, and now no matter what I tell him, he thinks he deserves to talk to me whenever he wants. He asked me out again over Thanksgiving, and I turned him down, and that just made him worse. He's started to . . . I just really, really needed him to go away. I told him that I like girls, and he didn't believe me, so I said I had a crush on one, and he asked who, and I didn't think you guys ever talked so I said your name. I'm so sorry."

Now it's my turn to blush. What Ella Quinn isn't saying is that she said my name because she knew no one was going to talk to me about it. She didn't think Tyler cared enough about me to tell me what she said. She didn't think I was enough of a person to worry about.

"I wouldn't have done it if I wasn't genuinely afraid of what Tyler might do otherwise," Ella Quinn says.

I don't think I've ever been this angry. Suddenly, on the hard blue plastic arena seat with the sound of kids squealing on the ice making my ears ring, I've had just about enough of Ella Quinn and Tyler and everyone else who thinks they see through me.

"What, so you decided if you gave him a new target, things would be easier for you? That's that, right? Who cares that the next target is a person with her own feelings?"

Ella Quinn tries to say something, but I cut her off. I'm pretty sure this is the most I've spoken so far this school year.

"And anyway, Tyler and I talk enough that I know you sucked as a girlfriend. I know all about how whiny you were and how you tried to get him to stop hanging out with his friends and how hard you cried when he dumped you. Why should I believe that Tyler's this big scary monster when he's been nothing but honest with me and all you've done is throw me under the bus?"

My phone buzzes. When I look down, my eyes are blurry and I blink hard to make sure I don't actually cry. *5 mins,* my dad says.

I know that I'm partially only mad because I'm embarrassed. I should never have told Ella Quinn about my sexuality; it's none of her business, first of all, and what made me think that the person I've spent a year hearing about being untrustworthy is actually trustworthy?

Ella Quinn is crying now, and I feel a little twinge, but I

ignore it. Even if everything she just said was true—which it isn't—I have every right to be mad at her.

I have every right to be mad at her.

I fly down the arena stairs and try to make myself as small as possible while I wait for my dad to pick me up outside. Neither of us says a word on the drive home.

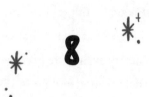

My parents don't drink very often, but I can tell when they've been drinking, because it's always on a Friday night, they always keep me up because my mom's laugh gets super loud, and they're always very, very quiet the next morning. They'll both have two painkillers with breakfast and then say something like *wouldn't visiting the library be fun today?* or *the mall will be way too busy this morning, we should wait it out.*

Basically, what I'm trying to say is I know what a hangover looks like, and I think now I know what one feels like, too.

Not that I was drinking or anything. It's just that when I got home last night I ran upstairs to my room and slammed the door shut so loudly that it woke up Rowan, and Rowan started screaming. My mom rushed over to his room and my dad went upstairs to help and while all of that was going on I took the big blue duvet off my bed and wrapped it all around me and sat in my closet even though I barely fit in there and cried and cried and cried.

Not my finest moment.

My parents came into my room to try and talk to me after

they got Rowan back down, but I hadn't been able to stop the tears and that just freaked them out even more. They ended up bringing me ice cream again and told me that, unless I was in big trouble, they trusted me to tell them what was wrong whenever I wanted. That made me cry even more because what if they already *knew* that of *course* their freak daughter is always going to be the butt of the joke? What if they were just humoring me?

I didn't stop crying until after midnight, so in the morning my eyes are stuck shut and my face is puffy and I'm so tired I almost nod off in the car on the way to school. My mom is back at work part time now, so some days are Mom days and some days are bus days. I can't decide which I would prefer right now.

"Is this what a hangover feels like?" I ask my mom.

She looks alarmed for a second, and then sees that I look like a rabid Muppet in a hoodie and bursts into laughter. She has little laugh lines around her eyes and I think they make her look smarter, like someone you're supposed to pay attention to.

"Honestly? Probably," she says. "You were up pretty late; you might be a little . . . dehydrated."

That's a pretty nice way of saying *you cried so much you might not have any water left in your whole body.*

"So I can stay home?" I ask hopefully, even though I know it's pointless since she has to work and we're already pulling into the school drop-off zone.

My mom pauses for a second. She knows as well as I do that if we stay in the drop-off zone for too long one of Jennifer Patel's dads is gonna start leaning on his horn, because they both take the drop-off zone Extremely Seriously.

"How about tonight we go out for dinner?" she asks. "Just us. We'll leave the boys at home and you can tell me what's been going on. Or you can just make me buy you a ridiculous dessert you'll be way too full to finish."

That doesn't sound *terrible*.

"Deal," I say, and jump out of the car just before the honking starts.

Riley is waiting for me in the yard, which brings me right back down to yesterday. I think I'm all cried out, but it still doesn't feel great to see one of Ella Quinn's best friends, who I'm sure must know everything that happened by now.

"Can we talk?" she asks.

"I'm not talking right now," I say. "The last time I tried, it didn't go very well. But I'm sure you know that."

"Ella's telling the truth," Riley says, rushing up to me, brandishing her phone. It's new, bigger than her whole hand, and gold. I have my mom's old phone and it's got this massive chunky case on it, so it doesn't even fit in my pockets. Riley's phone doesn't even have a case on it yet, and I wince at the thought of it shattering.

"Oh, thanks," I say. "That means a lot coming from such an impartial source."

"Please will you just look at this!" Riley says.

That's louder than I've ever heard her speak, I think. Riley is kind of like me, except instead of having to decide she was better off without friends, she had the advantage of a mom who's best friends with Ella Quinn's mom, so Ella Quinn lets her tag along on whatever grand adventures you have when you're Ella Quinn. Riley's quiet, but not in the way that makes people think she doesn't want any friends, like me. I don't know if that's because she's cracked the secret to getting everyone to like you in middle school or if Ella Quinn is telling everyone else to leave her alone.

Either way, Riley and I are similar enough that I know I should take her seriously when she explodes. I reach out and take her phone.

It's open to an account page on I Wonder, this app where you make an account and people can send you anonymous questions. It's supposed to be fun, like *Where did you get that shirt you were wearing today?* or *What's your favorite show right now?*

But it's anonymous, and we're in middle school, so you see where this is going.

"This is Ella's account," Riley says. She comes around to stand beside me so we can both look at the screen, where all of Ella Quinn's unanswered questions sit.

How does it feel to be such a slut?

Did u wear those shorts yesterday to show off ur fat ass?

There are more. There are so many more, and each of them is worse than the last. Some of them are rude, some of them are gross, some of them are *scary,* the kind of thing you have to hear about in those school assemblies about online safety and you think *no one* actually *sends messages like that* because they're so disgusting and detailed and vile. If I were Ella Quinn, I would never go to school again. I would throw out all my clothes and run away to the woods and become a witch. Even just reading the messages, knowing that people think like that about girls in *general*, makes me want to cover myself up.

"This has been going on since the summer," Riley says. "She's scared. Like, genuinely afraid."

I would be, too.

"But there's no proof that any of these are from Tyler," I say. "Like, they're horrible, but maybe they aren't from him? Anyone could find this account, right?"

Riley looks upset, but reluctantly nods.

"That's why she can't tell anyone," she says. "We don't have proof."

I'm about to say *oh, that's too bad! Sorry!* and walk away, but then I see it.

Down at the bottom, one of the first messages.

It's gonna be pretty diffecult for u to find a boyfriend who'll put up with u. ur body only gets u so far with a face that ugly.

Diffecult.

I know everything about Tyler Harris. I know that he cries at Disney movies and his first crush was on a picture of his mom's best friend in college. And I know that, no matter how hard he tries, he always, *always* misspells *difficult* as *diffecult*.

9

I can't stop staring at Tyler all morning.

He doesn't look at me, because he doesn't have any more secrets for me so there's nothing I can do for him or offer him. That's the thing about Tyler, I'm realizing: you only exist to him when he needs something, when you can carry his secrets or help him with math or listen while he complains to you about the girl he's harassing online while you just nod along like an idiot.

Just thinking about it, I practically drill a hole in the floor tapping my foot angrily.

Miss A gives us time to work on our speeches, but for the first time ever I don't even care about adding new ideas or practicing in my head or thinking about what the competition might be like. All of that seems like it lives in a totally different world now. Yesterday feels like months ago. All I can do is think about what Tyler is doing, and how I can make it stop. By the time the bell rings for lunch, I bump into the doorframe because I'm not paying any attention to where I'm going.

Lunch at Oakridge is weird. We don't have recess, but you're allowed to go outside whenever you want after you're finished eating. A lot of the older kids sneak their lunches outside and try to eat in the yard when it's nice out, and the cafeteria is suspiciously empty when I get there. I decide lunch can wait and instead wander outside to try to spot Tyler.

I don't know why I say *try to spot* Tyler, like he's a lion and I'm on a safari. Tyler always makes sure everyone knows where he is: he's the loudest, the fastest, the funniest. I don't know what he would do if he weren't those things. I don't think he knows, either.

"I need to talk to you," I say as soon as I see him.

Once I realize what I just did, though, my confidence wavers. I've never just marched up to Tyler Harris while he was being Tyler Harris, all sparkly and hilarious and the center of attention. A girl in the little group of people surrounding him arches her eyebrow at me like I'm trying to steal him from her, but joke's on her because I don't even know who she is and if Tyler was interested in her, he would have already whined about how hot he thinks she is to me for at least an hour. Tyler's best friend, Kaden, gives me a funny look and I try not to let it make me feel small, but it's hard not to feel small standing beside Kaden. He's almost six feet tall already and he got confused for a teacher by a substitute the other day. Last year there was a rumor going around that he was an undercover cop, but I'm basically positive that isn't true.

"Why?" Tyler says, laughing a little like the idea of talking to me is completely nuts. A few people laugh around him.

I lose my voice for a second. Everyone's staring at me. Somehow, I'm here, and I'm fully planning on saying some seriously crazy things. Things you're supposed to be 100 percent sure of before you say them. I'm only, like, 98 percent sure.

But then I remember that I'm not the type of person who gets nervous speaking in front of a crowd. When I'm giving a speech, I can be a totally different person, someone who isn't ever afraid of anything and who can stand up straight and tell people things they never knew before. I can make people listen to what I have to say.

I just need to be a different, slightly cooler version of that person.

"I'd be happy to talk about it in front of everyone if you want!" I chirp. "But I feel like you don't want that."

For a second, Tyler looks angry. He looks like the type of person who would tell Ella Quinn disgusting things about her boobs (but not use the word *boobs*) on I Wonder. I bring my level of sure up to 99 percent.

As quickly as that came, though, the anger smooths over.

"Fine," he says. Everyone's still laughing like it's all a big joke. How many of them know how Tyler spends his free time? Does he show them the messages? Do they all laugh along with him? Or would they be just as freaked out as I am? Everyone knows that Kaden can't keep his mouth shut (so he's definitely not a cop, then, now that I think about it). Would it be different if it were him telling Tyler to stop?

Tyler tries to drag me by the arm away from the group, but I snatch it back and lead the way over to a tree in the corner of the yard.

"Y'know people come back here to make out, right?" he asks, smirking. "People are gonna talk about you now. Is that what you wanted?"

"Shut up," I say. "Would you please just shut up for half a second? Just *one time* let me talk to you instead of you talking *at* me?"

I don't know where it comes from, but it feels really good to say.

Tyler raises an eyebrow at me, and then bows grandly.

"Please, my lady," he says. "State your business so we can get whatever this is over with."

"Are you sending those messages to Ella Quinn?"

Tyler freezes coming back up from his bow.

"No. What messages?"

He's lying.

"Those horrible, disgusting, *threatening* messages on her I Wonder? Those aren't you, mister diff-e-cult?"

Tyler knows that I've caught him. I kind of expect for him to tell me it was all a mistake, or a misunderstanding, or he meant to do it but now he feels awful and he needs my help to try to make things right with Ella Quinn. Instead, he just snorts.

"I guess that's my calling card," he says. "I'm like a Batman villain. If you're a big enough loser to remember it, that is."

"You aren't even going to *pretend* like you feel bad?" My mouth drops open.

"Why should I feel bad?" he asks. "Girls like Ella Quinn live for this kind of stuff. They just want attention, and I'm giving it to her. Now she gets to be all fake-weepy and act like a victim, and everyone will love her even more. I'm doing her a favor, really."

"You're doing her a *favor?*" My voice goes so high pitched and loud, a squirrel falls out of one of the trees nearby. "What on *earth* is she getting out of this? You can't seriously think that what you're doing is *fun* for her."

"If she's the kind of girl who's gonna pretend like she likes me and kiss me at the movies and then all of a sudden break up with me for *no* reason, then yeah, I'm pretty sure it is fun for her. You see the way she looks. She wouldn't dress like that if she didn't *love* having guys pay attention to her."

I have no idea what to say to that.

"You sound like one of those videos they play in health class!" I burst out. "Do you understand how gross and stupid you're being right now?"

Tyler laughs again, an ugly little snort that makes me clench my fists.

"Why have I never realized you were this terrible?" I ask "Why have you never treated *me* this badly?"

"Why would I?" He looks just as confused as me.

I realize what he means then. Because I'm not pretty like Ella Quinn. Because I don't have boobs like Ella Quinn. Because I don't laugh at his jokes or make him feel better about himself, I don't count. Why would he have to get my attention? Why would he ever want to make me notice him in that way?

You don't exist to Tyler unless you're helping him, or he likes looking at you. Now I won't exist to him at all.

"Leave Ella Quinn alone," I say.

"Why? Is she your girlfriend now?"

His lip curls up around the word *girlfriend*, and I can't take it anymore. I can't take him saying that and twisting it, making it something gross and shameful when I know, I *know* it's not. I can't take him getting away with everything just because he smiles nicely at teachers and wins ribbons on track and field day. I can't take it.

It's like it happens in slow motion. Something comes over me, and I lunge forward. I plant both of my hands on Tyler's shoulders, and I shove. He isn't expecting it, and he stumbles backwards until he lands butt-first in a puddle.

Tyler would never tell anyone that he got knocked down by a girl, especially not when the girl is me, so for a moment we just stare at each other, knowing the conversation is over.

Until I hear a whistle blowing.

Mr. Pitts comes stalking across the field, zeroing in on me. My blood runs cold as Tyler starts to smirk up at me.

Oakridge has a zero-tolerance policy for physical bullying.

Is this how it feels when you turn bad? Is this the beginning of my downward spiral?

"I'm sure I didn't see what I think I just saw," Mr. Pitts says. He has this habit of standing directly over kids, using his height to intimidate us in a way other adults never seem to notice.

"I fell," Tyler says immediately.

At first, I'm shocked that Tyler's covering for me, but then he cuts his eyes at me. Like he's saying *shut up*.

Of course Tyler's making excuses. Why would he ever want people to know that weird, friendless Hazel managed to push him hard enough that he fell right into the mud?

"Hazel put her hands on my shoulders and it surprised me," Tyler continues. "So I stepped backwards and tripped."

"And why were you putting your hands on his shoulders?" Mr. Pitts asks me.

Ugh, Tyler.

All three of us know why a boy and a girl might hide in the trees. There's *literally* a song about it. *Hazel and Tyler, sitting in a tree.*

"We were . . . playing tag," I say. It's weak, but it's something. "I got too excited when I caught up to him and used both hands, I guess."

Mr. Pitts obviously doesn't believe me, but he doesn't believe any kid when they tell him anything. He's one of those teachers who thinks kids are always trying to lie to him and cause trouble.

"It's true," Tyler says. "I'm fine, I swear."

"I'm sure you know about our school's policy against bullying," Pitts says to me.

If that were true, you wouldn't be teaching here, I think.

"She wasn't bullying me," Tyler insists. "I just fell."

"Still," Pitts says. "You should be more careful. Thankfully, you'll have plenty of time to rethink your tag strategy in detention, young lady."

Even though I know Pitts is being unfair, that he's on some kind of power trip and as far as he knows I didn't do anything wrong, it still freaks me out. I *should* try to summon whatever made me stand up to Tyler and stand up to Pitts, but this is different. Tyler's annoying, but Mr. Pitts is an actual teacher. He can put me in detention for no reason if he wants to. What makes someone think they can treat people like that?

And then Tyler mouths *you owe me* as Pitts marches me away, and I think I get it. Tyler Harrises grow up to be Mr. Pittses.

10

I've never gotten detention before.

I don't think anyone's ever paid attention to me long enough to give me detention. Sometimes if Tyler is talking to me, a teacher will give us a look to get him to stop, but they've never actually said anything, and they've *definitely* never given me detention over it. A lot of teachers have these lists in their head: Good Kids and Bad Kids. It's really hard to switch lists. I figured out in elementary school that every teacher has a "well of patience" for you. If you keep it full by doing stuff like answering questions and smiling at them in the hall and laughing at their jokes even if they aren't very funny, you can get away with more stuff. You just need to figure out what fills each teacher's well, and how much you can put in it without becoming a suck-up.

Last year, for example, Mrs. Noble didn't care that I read in the middle of lectures, because I could still answer her geography questions and half the class was running an illegal Pokémon gambling ring, so she had bigger fish to fry. All I needed to do was be better than *those* kids and she was perfectly happy with me.

Mr. Pitts is one of those teachers where some parents say he's *firm, but fair,* except all of the kids say he's *just super mean* and *he threw a* chair, *are you serious?* He patrols the yard in a windbreaker and reflective sunglasses, and I imagine that if I had a friend, I'd tell them that he looks like a mall cop and we'd both laugh at him as he marched by, whistle in hand, ready to ruin a kid's life at a moment's notice.

On the first day of school this year, I saw at least three kids crying when they realized he was going to be their teacher. But he's been a teacher for at least a million years, so it's not like he's going anywhere. I don't know what I would have done if he was my homeroom teacher. Sometimes he teaches us gym and that's *more* than enough for me, thank you.

Pitts's well of patience is pretty much nonexistent, so he doesn't care about *how* Tyler ended up on the ground as much as he cares about the fact that there was someone around to blame for it. He thinks all kids are evil creatures who absolutely cannot be trusted until they're at least thirty. Thus, detention.

I thought that I would be more upset—of course Tyler gets away with everything while I'm enjoying some quality time with Mr. Pitts—but I don't really care. Violence is never the answer and blah blah blah, but I have to admit it felt pretty good to see the look on Tyler's face when he realized I was being serious. That he was going to pay attention to what I had to say.

Tyler's long gone now. He ran back to his little group of friends and no doubt is going to spend the rest of the day telling them what a freak I am. But I don't really care about that either, since he's also going to have to spend the rest of the day in wet, muddy jeans that have a giant brown stain on the butt. Mr. Pitts is still very much here, though, and he whips out a thin rectangular pad of paper from his shirt pocket.

"Your parents are going to need to initial this," he says, not looking at me as he checks boxes on the pad and then signs off on it with a flourish. "You can bring it to the teacher on detention duty tomorrow at lunch."

I get the feeling "teacher" wasn't Mr. Pitts's first choice career path, but I don't want to ask him if he got kicked out of police school and risk getting expelled myself.

"Thanks," I say, and go to take the slip from him. He yanks it out of my reach so I'm grasping at nothing, pauses for a second with the slip held up high, and then finally smirks and passes it over. He walks away, and I'm left wishing I could push him in a puddle, too. Maybe some people just need to spend a day in dirty jeans.

My mom picks me up after school and takes me right to this little restaurant in town that we used to go to before Rowan was born (I'm starting to realize how often I think about things that happened Before Rowan Was Born). It's barely four p.m., but my mom just calls it the early-bird special like we're in on a joke together and it makes me smile despite the day I had. All the other diners are about eighty years old. Every one of them looks like they'd pinch my cheeks if given the opportunity. I duck my head so as not to tempt them.

When we go to sit, Mom barely has her mouth open to ask me about my day before I burst out, "So I got detention today."

My mom's eyebrows fly up. I think she's just as confused about what to do about this as I am, honestly. What's she going to do, ground me? Oh no, I can't hang out with the friends I don't have!

"Do you want to talk about what happened?" she asks.

I think about it. I'm pretty sure my mom would be happy to hear that I was standing up for someone else, that I knew something had to be done, so I did it. I don't know if she would be as excited if she found out exactly what I did. I also don't know if she would believe what's going on. I mean, I was skeptical initially. My mom's never even met Tyler. Why would she believe that he sucks as much as he does when no other adult in the school seems to get it? Plus, parents have this weird network that you can never be too sure about. Sometimes I think my mom has no idea who someone is, and then their name comes up and it's all *oh of course, their mom was my roommate in college!* out of nowhere. What if she's friends with Tyler's mom, and she makes me do something really embarrassing that she read in a parenting book like write him a letter or spend a day volunteering with him so we learn to see past our differences? (I've found it's very useful to secretly read my parents' parenting books. The more I can do to be one step ahead of them, the better.)

"A boy in my class was being rude to my friend and I told him to stop," I eventually say.

The *my friend* part slips out. I really, *really* don't think Ella Quinn and I count as friends. Yesterday was the most I've ever spoken to her and that ended with both of us crying. But my mom's face lights up at the idea. She doesn't seem to care about the fact that I'm being super vague about what actually happened. I said the magic word: friend.

"Good for you!" she says. "I think that's great. I'm sure you've realized that whatever you did *after* you asked him to stop might not have been the best idea?"

To be honest, no, but I know what she wants to hear, and if I want her to let it go, I'll need to say it. Parents have wells of patience, too.

"Definitely."

My mom nods slowly. "Do we need to talk about anything that might be going on at school?" she asks carefully.

Probably.

"Do you think I could try to handle this myself?" I ask. "If anything else happens, I'll let you know. But for now, I think I've got this."

My mom hesitates for a second, so I add, "No more detention, promise. But you *do* have to sign this."

I hand the slip over to my mom—just hand it to her, without faking her out, *Mr. Pitts*—and she looks it over for a long time.

Eventually, she nods slowly. "No more detention. If it happens again, your dad and I are gonna need to get involved. But for now, I trust you. I'm sure you can get this figured out." She signs the slip and passes it back to me.

I'm sure of that too, which is kind of unexpected. I don't think you're supposed to find your purpose when you get too angry and shove a gross guy in your class to the ground, but that's kind of what it feels like.

My mom and I both order desserts we can't finish, bring them home, and eat the leftovers together on the couch.

11

Detention isn't as bad as I thought it would be for three reasons:

1. When I walk into the classroom at lunch, I fully expect to see Mr. Pitts there, possibly with some kind of evil mustache he grew overnight, definitely in a swivel chair with a hairless cat on his lap, ready to tell me that I was going to spend an hour clapping erasers. (Admittedly, most of my knowledge of detention comes from TV shows. I don't even really know what "clapping erasers" means. We have Smart Boards.) Instead, Miss A is sitting at the desk at the front of the room, and she appears to be knitting. It's hard to feel intimidated by a person who's knitting. (Though I wouldn't want to see those needles in Mr. Pitts's hands.)

2. The rest of the classroom is empty, which is good because the other scenario I'd conjured up involved me being stuck with a bunch of kids in nonvegan leather jackets who would peer pressure me into experimenting with

drugs. Then I would fall in with The Wrong Crowd and probably end up robbing a bank, y'know, to get drugs, and my parents would be interviewed on the local news saying they always knew there was something off about me. (I think that particular scenario comes from those health class warning videos.)

3. Miss A smiles when she sees me. And when I tentatively sit down at a desk in the middle of the room, she tells me that I should work quietly on anything school-related I need to get done with a little smirk like she knows that's not much of a punishment for me. Then she returns to her knitting. I think it's a hat, but it also might be booty shorts. Only time will tell, I guess.

Even though I'm still thinking about the way Tyler looked at me yesterday—like I was nothing, like I didn't deserve his time, like I didn't deserve *anyone's* time—I know that I need to actually take advantage of an uninterrupted work period, for once. Without Tyler here to try to ruin my day, or Ella Quinn here to remind me of how badly I embarrassed myself, I actually have a chance to whip my speech even more into shape.

The first competition round is less than three weeks away, which means Ella Quinn can probably already say hers backwards and forwards and in her sleep. If I beat her during the first round, which takes place in the gym in front of the whole school, then I'll move on to a regional competition in the new year. I heard that they give the contestants free doughnuts there; it's the big leagues.

The mysteries I was using before weren't cool enough. I've pinned down the "it factor"—you need to also be a little bit freaked out. Kids love scary stuff. I think I've finally settled on my new mysteries. I'm keeping the Black Dahlia, but adding Jack the Ripper and the *Mary Celeste*—the name of a ship that was found floating around in the ocean with no crew. The speech has to be at least three minutes long but no longer than five, so I figure if you include an intro and outro that gives me plenty of time to talk about all of the mysteries without going overboard (which, by the way, is one of the theories about the crew of the *Mary Celeste*. I laugh at my own joke, but then Miss A looks up at me and tilts her head confusedly, so I put my head back down).

I can't practice my speech out loud, but I know that I'll get bonus points for having it memorized, so I take out my notebook and try to write it from memory. I make it all the way up until halfway through the Jack the Ripper portion before I need to check my notes. Last year I couldn't go ten seconds without looking down at my cue cards, so I sit up a little straighter in my seat. Ella Quinn is going down, cool speech about poison or not.

At the reminder of Ella Quinn, though, I slump a little. I know I need to apologize to her, and definitely soon, for not believing what she said about Tyler. I keep thinking about how scared she looked. How upset she was that I didn't believe her. I go red thinking about what I said to Riley, implying that Ella Quinn was exaggerating the weird things older guys said to her because of the way she looks.

I'd told Tyler he'd been acting like a bad health class movie yesterday, but I haven't been much better. Honestly, now I feel a little stupid for thinking that Tyler would tell me the truth about *anything*, let alone about Ella Quinn. Why would he feel the need to be honest about her when he goes back and forth between loving and hating her every other day?

I open up a new page in my notebook and start jotting down some apology points. Not having friends is usually great because it means I'm never fighting with anyone, which also means I never have to apologize to anyone. I might be a little rusty, so if I'm going to do this, it's good to prepare in advance.

* Ella Quinn deserved to be believed when she told me she was afraid of someone who was sexually harassing her.

(I write *sexually harassing* in really small letters, like it's being whispered. As if Miss A would be able to tell what I was writing and leap into action.)

* Even though I don't think it was right of her to tell Tyler she had a crush on me, she didn't know that I am actually gay, so I don't think that's too much her fault. As far as she knew, I was just someone Tyler didn't care about and who would never hear about any of this. At least she was right on the first part, I guess.
* I *did* try to defend her once I realized the truth.
* I should also probably apologize to Riley.

"Hazel," Miss A says, making me jump. I forgot where I was for a second, which only happens when I'm too deep in thought to pay attention to the other stuff.

"Sorry," I say automatically.

"What for?" she asks. "I mean, besides the thing that got you here in the first place, of course."

I wasn't sure if Miss A actually knew why I was in detention, but I guess it makes sense that she does. I grimace, except I don't actually feel too bad about the whole thing.

Thinking about Tyler almost makes me snap my pen, but I'm pretty sure even Miss A would have some questions if I did that (and anyway, I'm wearing a white shirt today and that just spells disaster). He wasn't in class this morning, and when Miss A called his name, Kaden turned around from his seat in the front of the room and stared at me. I can't figure out what it was supposed to mean. I don't think he looked angry, exactly, but I have to assume he isn't my biggest fan right now. Best friend code and all that crap.

"I don't know, actually," I say to Miss A.

"You should never apologize if you don't know what you're apologizing for," she says. "You should always think very carefully before you say you're sorry, or it'll lose its meaning. And then where will we be?"

I can't tell if she's quizzing me on history or trying to impart an important life lesson. Sometimes she tries to do both at once and I'm not sure if anyone gets it.

"Good point," I say noncommittally, and she seems to like that, giving me a nod.

"I'm supposed to keep you here for another twenty minutes," Miss A says. "But between you and me, I think it's ridiculous that they take away your entire lunch hour. Why don't you head out a little early? If you see Mr. Pitts, tell him I'm entirely to blame."

She winks at me. Or, at least I think she tries to wink at me. Both of her eyes close, but one closes a little more than the other. I can't really wink either, so I appreciate the effort.

"Thank you!" I say, and hurry to pack up my stuff. Tyler isn't here today, so getting out early is even better. No one's around to ruin my day.

"Say hi to your friends for me," Miss A says, and I stop.

It's no secret that I don't have friends. It's the one thing teachers always say at parent-teacher meetings. *Hazel is such a star student, such a great help around the class . . . socially, she's still a little in her shell!*

Is she trying to be mean? Is she making fun of me?

I scrunch my face up, trying to figure out what she meant by that, but when I open the door and walk out into the hall, Ella Quinn and Riley are leaning up against the lockers across from the detention room, and both of them are grinning at me.

Before I even know what I'm doing, I'm grinning back.

12

"She let you out early!" Ella Quinn says when she sees me, as if this is normal, as if I get detention all the time and Ella Quinn and Riley are always waiting for me when I'm dismissed. "I love Miss A, you're so lucky to have her and not that awful old man."

Ella Quinn starts walking, and when Ella Quinn walks, she walks like she's very used to people following along behind her, so Riley and I do exactly that.

"I'm sorry," I blurt out, except Ella Quinn says the same thing at the exact same time. She laughs, and I kind of smile.

"I'll go first," she says. "I'm sorry about what happened to you yesterday. And I'm sorry about what I said the day before. And I'm sorry about all the other times I'm sure Tyler told you terrible things about me. It wasn't right for me to use your name like that, and I'm sorry Tyler dragged you into this in the first place. I should have thought about how it would affect you."

I kind of get what Miss A was just talking about, now. You can tell when someone put thought into saying sorry, and Ella Quinn's been thinking a lot about this apology.

"That's okay," I say, and I mean it. "I'm sorry that I freaked out on you. I should have believed you right away, especially over *Tyler.*"

When I say his name Ella Quinn and Riley both make matching disgusted noises.

"And I'm sorry I didn't get to see Tyler fall on his ass yesterday," Riley says, and it surprises me so much that I laugh louder than I think I ever have in public.

My laugh is super loud normally, but only my parents (and Rowan, I guess) have ever really heard it. It sounds like a donkey, and I've never had to be self-conscious of it until now.

Ella Quinn and Riley laugh, but not in a mean way. I think we're all still laughing about Tyler falling, and it makes my fingertips kind of tingle to be included.

"Mr. Pitts called me *young lady*," I say. "Like we were in some finishing school somewhere."

"Do *not* get Ella started on finishing schools," Riley says. "It's like her biggest dream to go to one."

"It is *not!*" Ella Quinn says. "I just read a lot of old books and everyone's always going to finishing schools in them, and they seem like really fancy places where you get to go to tons of balls and then rich guys offer to, like, *buy* you from your dad so then you have to go on some kind of adventure where you escape on a pirate ship or enlist the help of ancient demons or something. I'm only interested in the first and last parts, not so much the middle."

We all laugh again, but it's embarrassing to me that I hadn't considered Ella Quinn would read a bunch. I guess when Tyler told me she was stupid, I believed him, but that doesn't even make *sense* because I know that *I'm* not stupid and she beat me in the speech competition.

"Have you eaten lunch yet?" Ella Quinn asks me after a minute.

I shake my head. "I have a super-boring sandwich, but I had to go straight to detention at lunch, so."

"It's wild that they don't even let you eat lunch," Riley says. "How is that not illegal?"

Ella Quinn snorts.

"They make us run until we puke in gym, you think they care if Hazel eats her sandwich?"

Riley rolls her eyes, but not in the same way I've seen other girls roll their eyes at Ella Quinn. It's not the usual annoyance at someone so loud, someone who always knows the answer and who isn't afraid to say it, or to tell someone when they got it wrong. It's more of a laugh, an inside joke, and for the first time I feel like I'm inside it, too.

"I can eat wherever," I say.

I don't know why I say that. We're only allowed to eat in the cafeteria—bringing snacks outside is a surefire way to get yelled at or put straight back into detention. A lot of the older kids (and some of the younger kids who want to be cool, like Tyler) sneak their food outside in their coat pockets and eat under the trees, passing Fruit Roll-Ups back and forth like they're black-market pangolins or something.

Ella Quinn gives me a look and a gentle laugh.

"All right, Bonnie Parker," she says. "You only just got *out* of detention—it feels like my duty as a friend to put a stop to this life of crime before it goes any further."

1. Who's Bonnie Parker?
2. Her duty as a friend?

I don't want to make it weird and be like, *friend?* And then have her be like, *yeah, friends,* and then have some kind of mortifyingly cheesy happy ending because a) I want to be a little bit cooler than *that,* at least, and b) the ending can't be that happy because Tyler Harris is still harassing Ella Quinn, and I'm not okay with that just fading into the background.

Ella Quinn leads us into the cafeteria, which is pretty empty by now since everyone usually powers through their lunch to get outside before all the good spots are taken (there are like ten thousand kids in this school and only four benches outside, which I will never understand). There are a few people dotted around— it's either the ones who care too much, sitting by the windows surrounded by books and talking about which high school they're going to go to and then which college after that, or the ones who don't care at all, sleeping with their cheeks squished against the yellowish vinyl cafeteria tables. When it starts to get *really* cold, there's usually a third group: people who don't want to freeze their fingers off outside. That group gets bigger the snowier it gets. They're all pretending to study at one of the tables.

The cafeteria is actually kind of nice right now. It's quiet, and it smells like french fries but not in a gross way, and the sun isn't right above the school anymore so the light's streaming in through the long narrow windows and turning everything kind of dreamy and glowy.

"I love coming in here after everyone leaves," Ella Quinn says, reading my mind. "No one bothers anyone and no one's screaming about fish sticks."

I snort. Someone actually *did* start screaming about fish sticks the other day.

"I hope you don't mind that we're following you around," Ella Quinn says.

Riley goes red. "We're not following her around," she says, elbowing her.

"You are a little, I guess," I say. "But I don't mind."

Ella Quinn elbows Riley back.

"I just wanted to make sure that we're okay," Ella Quinn says. "I know we aren't, like, best friends or anything, but I feel really bad that I dragged you into all of this and then you got in trouble because of me, basically."

"Definitely because of you," Riley says to her.

I've never given Riley much thought beyond she's-Ella-Quinn's-best-friend, but I decide that I like her. I thought she would be following Ella Quinn around, not wanting to make her mad and obeying her every command, but that's not what Riley's like. That's not what *they* are like. I think I might actually like what they're like.

"Do you have plans for the weekend?" Ella Quinn asks me

as soon as I take a bite out of my sandwich. My lunches have been more and more boring ever since Rowan was born.

That feels like a very grown-up question to ask a person, like maybe Ella Quinn thinks I'll respond *oh yes, my wife and I are going to the farmers' market to pick up fresh produce for the dinner party we're hosting on Saturday night.* I don't think I have any big, exciting plans, but I'm not one of those people who sits at home and thinks about how I don't have any plans and feels sorry for myself. My plans for the weekend are to work on my speech and watch a lot of TV, and I'm pretty happy with them.

"Not really," I say, instead of saying all of that.

Ella Quinn looks a little shy suddenly, picking at a spot on the table and fidgeting in her seat.

"Just 'cause Riley's sleeping over tomorrow night, and we thought if you weren't doing anything you might want to come too? But don't worry if you can't! We can do it another time. Or not at all, if you'd rather just forget all of this happened."

It's very, very weird to see Ella Quinn nervous.

"I could probably do that," I say.

13

My parents basically lose their minds when I ask them if I can sleep over at Ella Quinn's house during dinner on Friday night. I could have asked them on Thursday, when Ella Quinn asked me, but I've found that sometimes you have to just spring things on my parents. If I'd asked on Thursday, I would have had to deal with my mom pretending like she wasn't way too excited for me for the whole day today.

"Of course!" my mom says. Her face looks like it's going to crack in half. She's trying not to smile because she knows that would make her look too excited and she doesn't want to scare me off, but also, she can't stop the smile. I look down at the kitchen table, which is covered in scratches and dents and dots of permanent marker because, as my parents love telling me, this table was the first thing they bought together as a couple. I can only imagine the things it's seen.

"If you were that worried about me being some kind of friendless loser, you could have said something earlier," I say down to the table. My hair falls forward and covers half my face, but I don't try to move it.

"I don't think you're a friendless loser!" my mom says.

Well, shrieks.

"We'd never think that," my dad says. "We're just excited for you! You know that I'm still in touch with a lot of my friends from middle school. You're just figuring out who you are! Everything's so exciting! It's a great time to meet people you really get along with, and I just didn't want you to miss out on that."

My dad gets that hazy Glory Days look about him, so my mom knows that it's up to her to really bring this pep talk home.

"But we would never think you're a *loser!* If you want to hang out in your room all day every day and only come out for meals and the occasional shower, that's up to you. But we'd miss you. And your room might get smelly. But that would be your call!"

Seven out of ten. A pep talk lacking some pep. Generally underwhelmed, but I do appreciate the effort, and I didn't think my parents *actually* thought I was a loser anyway.

On cue, Rowan starts crying from the baby monitor sitting on the kitchen table. It has a little screen where you can watch him and the night vision always makes him look like a demon. His eyes are glowing in the monitor, which is fitting because he certainly *sounds* possessed with the way he's screaming. Sometimes I don't think he'll ever be old enough to *not* scream like that all the time.

"Of course you can sleep over at your friend's house," my mom says before she rushes up, and then it's just me and my dad.

"So is this the same Ella Quinn from the other night?" he asks.

"No," I say. "There are forty girls in my grade, but actually thirty-nine of them are named Ella Quinn. It's super weird."

"They warned me this day would come." My dad sighs. "They said when we had our beautiful baby girl, *just you wait, one day she'll be a teenager and she'll only ever be sarcastic,* and I said, *no, not* my *baby girl, never Hazel.* But here we are! The day has come!"

I raise an eyebrow at him.

"Are you done?" I ask.

My dad clears his throat. "Done."

I laugh a little. "Yeah, it's the same Ella Quinn from the other night," I say.

"Do I need to be on standby again?"

I think about it, but not for very long. "I don't think so. What happened at the arena was sort of a misunderstanding? There was more to it than I thought. So I don't think what happened then would happen tonight."

My dad nods, and I pick at my mostly finished dinner for a minute before my dad speaks up again.

"Do you want me to help you pack?" he asks.

"No, I do not."

"It'll be fun!"

"Will it?"

"Well, I've never been to a middle school girls' sleepover—"

"That's probably for the best."

"*But* from what I gather, there will likely be fashion shows. I am, of course, extremely fashionable."

My dad is wearing a shirt with a cartoon dog on it and there's a hole in the armpit so big you can see his stomach.

I go upstairs to pack, hoping all the while that there isn't, in fact, a fashion show element to this sleepover.

Ella Quinn's house is even more ridiculous up close than it is from the safe distance of the bus.

Her driveway alone takes ages to drive down all the way, winding through grassy fields in pitch black. It's dark enough that it makes me think about what could be out there. I shudder and hope I'll stop feeling this weird itchy discomfort at some point in the night. My parents might not think I'm a loser, but I'd definitely think less of myself if I chickened out of this sleepover.

I haven't been to a sleepover since elementary school, when the worst thing that would happen is someone would get homesick and leave early, or maybe someone's parents would yell at us for staying up past ten thirty p.m. Sleepovers back then were usually reserved for birthday parties or when someone else's parents were babysitting you. Since we've been in middle school, it's a whole other story. Now, every Monday it seems like there's some new drama or issue or fight that started at a Friday night sleepover.

People are always texting people super late at night or asking each other out at three a.m. and then pretending like they did it in their sleep. Or they have these big, massive friendship-ending fights that probably could have been resolved if everyone would just go to sleep. I don't know how prepared I am to be involved in these activities.

Ella Quinn's mom is standing in the door when my dad and I finally pull up to the front of the house. She's wearing maroon leggings and a very soft-looking white sweater. Her blond hair is piled up on top of her head, pushed away from her face with a soft fabric headband. She looks way younger than most of the parents around here, but then again, I only ever see other parents at drop-off when everyone's stressed out and just trying to get out of there. Ella Quinn's mom looks like she was supposed to be famous but then decided that whole scene wasn't for her and her fans respected her even more for it.

"It's so nice to finally meet you in person!" Ms. Quinn says, touching my shoulder. She and my dad do that *hello nice to meet you, you seem normal, that's great* conversation grownups do over my head and Ella Quinn comes downstairs.

Ella Quinn's hair is usually in a French braid (two if it's a special occasion), but now it's down. Her hair is curlier than it was on skate night, and it's all scraggly around her face. Usually I don't get that weird obsession adults seem to have about saying *you look just like your mom!* about kids, but *whoa*. Ella Quinn looks *just like* her mom.

"I've got it from here!" she says before her mom can talk

to me again. I turn around for one last glimpse at my dad and he mouths *fashion show* and I scowl at him, but then Ella Quinn grabs my arm to drag me upstairs and I laugh before I can help myself.

Ella Quinn's room isn't what I thought it would look like. I've never given it much thought, but on the drive here I was imagining some kind of huge room with high ceilings and a four-poster bed, maybe with some posters of her own face or rhinestones spelling out her name across the wall. Instead, it's light green, and her bedding is clean and white. There's a corkboard on the wall where concert tickets and pictures of Ella Quinn and Riley making silly faces are pinned up around a calendar open to last month's page. She has a space heater that keeps everything feeling cozy.

I think I was expecting somewhere I'd be uncomfortable, I realize. But I'm not uncomfortable here at all.

"Riley's gonna be here in a little while," Ella Quinn says once the door is shut and we're alone. "I asked her to come an hour after you."

"Oh," I say, because I don't really know how I'm supposed to react to that.

"I just know that it can be kind of weird to walk into a friendship, y'know? I didn't want you to feel like you were intruding or anything."

Ella Quinn's parents moved from the city the summer before middle school. We both got to Oakridge without many friends, but Ella Quinn had Riley, and then it seemed like it took no effort at all for her to have everyone else, too. I hadn't really thought about what that would have felt like; she never made it seem like she was worried about coming here or making friends, she just came here and made friends.

"Thank you," I say. I squirm a little and we both go quiet.

If this is what the rest of the night is going to feel like, I might be that elementary school kid who has to leave early. Heck, I might even be the one who *suggests a fashion show.*

"Have you had dinner yet, Hazel?" Ella Quinn's mom pokes her head through the door.

"Why did we get me the doorbell, Mom?" Ella Quinn asks.

"So I would stop barging in on you and Riley when you're having super-secret important conversations," she says. "I never agreed I'd do the same with you and *Hazel.*"

Now that she's pointed it out, I notice a little white wire coming from the other side of Ella Quinn's door. That's *genius.* I want one.

"We're going to have to revisit that agreement," Ella Quinn says.

"I've had dinner," I say, because it seems like Ella Quinn and her mom could go on like this for a while.

"I haven't," Ella Quinn says. "Hazel, what's it like to have a mother who provides for you?"

She says it so seriously that for a second I'm taken aback, but then Ella Quinn and her mom both start laughing.

"So hard done by," she says. "No one understands the cruelty you've been subjected to."

Ella Quinn flops backwards down onto her bed with her hand over her face.

"My life is extremely difficult."

"I know," her mom says. "But I think the gigantic pizza I just ordered might help a little."

Ella Quinn peeks out from under her hand. "Well, it can't hurt."

14

In hindsight, it was a bad idea to eat two slices of pizza on top of dinner.

Riley arrived at the same time as the pizza and Ella Quinn's mom said we could eat in her room, so now we're all sitting on the floor around the box like something out of the world's most wholesome movie. It's nice, but I need to remember to stay sharp. The potential for a fashion show is only increasing.

"I think the whole problem with him," Ella Quinn says, "is no one's ever told him *no* before."

We're talking about Tyler, because obviously we're talking about Tyler. Ella Quinn started by saying we shouldn't talk about him, that tonight was about hanging out and not thinking about Tyler Harris, but I'm finding the thing about hanging out with other girls is that it's super easy to talk about guys who've done gross things to us because, as it turns out, a lot of guys have done a lot of gross things. I know there's that joke about how girls at sleepovers only talk about boys, but I'm not quite sure if this is what people mean by that.

"His mom is, like, obsessed with him," Ella Quinn continues. "She thinks he's never done anything wrong in his whole life. When we went to the movies that one time, she sat in the row behind us and kept telling me I shouldn't have my ears pierced because *Tyler likes nice, clean-cut girls.* She would never in a million years think he spends all his free time terrorizing *nice, clean-cut girls.*"

"He thinks his mom is too involved in his life," I say automatically.

Ella Quinn and Riley look at me for a long beat, and I remember that I know a lot about Tyler Harris.

"He loves her," I continue. He hasn't explicitly said that to me, but it's obvious. "He never wants to complain about her too much, but you can tell he gets annoyed with how perfect she thinks he is."

They're still looking at me like I grew a second head.

"How often do you actually talk to Tyler?" Ella Quinn asks me.

I don't really feel like I need to lie this time. I don't need to downplay how often Tyler talks to me and what he says. He clearly doesn't care about me, so I'm not going to care about him. And once I realize that, it's like the gates open up.

"Like, all the time, I guess," I say. "He won't talk to his friends about his feelings and he won't tell any girl he might like one day, so I'm pretty much the only person he knows who won't tell his secrets to anyone else. I realized the other day that he does it because he thinks I'm not worthy of having a crush on myself, y'know? He wouldn't dare say anything to a girl he thinks is hot because then one day he'd have no one to confide in. I'm a safe bet, so he tells me *a lot of stuff*."

Ella Quinn and Riley give each other a look.

"I didn't, like, know that he was doing any of this," I add quickly. The last thing I need is for Ella Quinn and Riley to think I was laughing along with Tyler while he was sending all of those messages and harassing Ella Quinn. "He just tells me whatever he feels like telling me, but never enough that I could use any of it against him, really. Like, when you think about it, what's the worst that could happen if I told some random girl Tyler Harris has a crush on her? Nine times out of ten she'd be thrilled."

"So you're like a spy," Riley says.

I laugh. I'm surprised to feel so relieved that they aren't mad at me for knowing so much about the inner workings of Tyler Harris's mind.

"I'm basically a spy," I agree. "A really ineffective, accidental spy."

"Maybe you could tell me why Duncan White is being so obnoxious then," Riley says. "We're partners for a science project and he left me to do the whole thing."

"Ooh," I say before I can help myself, because I *do* actually know that one.

"You're kidding me." Riley laughs. "What about the part where you just said you were an *ineffective* spy?"

"Duncan's probably being weird because he used to have a crush on you, plus his parents are fighting about whether his mom should take a new job in Montana," I say. "But also, he kind of sucks, so I wouldn't go too easy on him just because of that. Last year he was supposed to be watching his little sister and she ended up spilling hot water from the stove all over herself. She was fine, but Tyler said Duncan doesn't even feel bad about it."

Riley blinks at me. For a second, I'm worried that she's offended that I may have overshared about someone's life when Duncan doesn't even really know me. And then I'm worried that Ella Quinn and Riley are going to start thinking I'm some kind of Boy Bible and decide I'm only good for telling them what boys are thinking. And then I kind of scare myself because I wonder if that would be the worst thing, really, to have this even if they saw me as a service and not a person.

But then Riley folds over laughing, hiding her face in her hands.

"He *liked* me?" she asks. "Is that why he got so awkward when I said I could go over to his house to work on the project? That's so *ridiculous*."

I thought it was ridiculous too, but I didn't think Riley would. I start to smile.

"Oh my god," Ella Quinn says. "Ri, that was why he kept trying to hang out with me and Tyler last year! He wanted to, like, get *intel*."

"I think you're taking the spy thing a little too far," Riley says, but she's still laughing.

"That was what he was doing, though," I say. "It annoyed Tyler *so* much, he almost stopped talking to Duncan completely."

"Do you have an I Wonder, Hazel?" Ella Quinn asks, looking up from her phone.

I shake my head. "My parents won't let me," I say, even though that's not true. If I asked, they'd probably say yes — they'd have no idea what I was talking about, but they'd most likely be fine with it once I assured them it wasn't some kind of drug — it just never seemed like something that would do me any good. Every time I considered getting one, I would just think about how it would feel if no one wondered anything about me, if no one really cared enough to ask me a question. Now I know that's not even the worst thing that could happen on there.

"I didn't tell my mom I was getting one," Ella Quinn says. She rolls her eyes at herself. "Don't tell her I said this, but now I kind of wish I had asked her for one and that she'd told me no. We would have fought, but then I would have gotten over it and this would never be happening."

"You and I both know that if she'd said you couldn't have an I Wonder you would have gotten one anyway," Riley says. "It's not your fault Tyler's doing this, and he's not doing this because you have an I Wonder. That's like saying it's someone's fault their house got broken into because they have a house."

I *definitely* like Riley. She doesn't put up with anything she doesn't like and she seems to really care about Ella Quinn. I think there would be worse people to have in your corner.

"It just sucks that I ever liked him in the first place," Ella Quinn says. Riley gives her a *look* and she laughs and waves her hands in front of her face. "Last time I mention him, I promise! I just feel stupid."

"You shouldn't feel stupid," I say. "He should feel stupid."

"It's not even that he should feel stupid!" Riley says. "He should be *in trouble*. But Tyler Harris is perfect as far as any adult in a ninety-mile radius is concerned, so he'll *never* get in trouble. I don't want to say this, Ella, but the only way you'll stop getting those messages is if you just delete your I Wonder all together."

We all think about that for a second. It's one thing to know that something's not fair, but it's entirely another to accept that.

"Fine," Ella Quinn says eventually, picking up her phone again and scrolling to the app. There's something scratching at the back of my head, a little thought that I can't quite hear yet.

Ella Quinn taps to delete the app and a notification pops up that says *Are you sure? Deleting I Wonder will delete all app data. All questions and answers will be lost.*

"Wait!" I smack Ella Quinn's phone out of her hand before she can do anything. "If you delete it, then we have no proof. Then it's like it never happened. Then he could . . ."

I trail off, but Riley's biting her lip like she knows where I was headed.

"Then he could do it to someone else," she says, and I nod.

But it's worse than that. I don't say it, but I know it.

I kept track, and Tyler Harris has told me about having crushes on twenty-seven different girls.

Has Tyler done *this* to 67.5 percent of the girls in our grade?

15

I've never really been one of those kids who hates going to school. I've always been good at school, so what was the point of avoiding it? Now I think I'm realizing that even though I've never *hated* it, I also never really looked forward to going. School was just somewhere I went, and I liked it enough, but I never spent a Sunday night unable to sleep because I couldn't wait to go the next day or anything like that. I've never been one of those kids who jumps out of the car to go and see their friends, or who talks about everything that happened at school with their parents at dinner. Up until now, school has just been school, the same way the sky's just been the sky.

When my dad drops me off on Monday morning, I think I'm actually excited about being at school.

My dad doesn't drop me off very often, but if it's supposed to be a Mom day and Rowan kept my mom up all night, like today, sometimes Dad swoops in. I don't always love it, because he always gets in trouble at the drop-off line. He says that us finishing our conversation is more important than "obeying The Man" and rushing. I swear sometimes I can see smoke coming out of Jennifer Patel's dad's ears when he realizes it's my dad driving me. I think that's why Mom doesn't let him do it very often.

Today, though, I dart across the seat to give him a quick hug and then leap out of the car so quickly, I have to turn around and grab my backpack because I almost forget it. My dad rolls down the window and yells something that sounds suspiciously like *Enjoy your fashion show!* at my back.

But it turns out that I ran all the way to the yard for nothing, because when I finally get there, I see almost everyone running around and finding their friends and talking about everything they did on the weekend. Everyone except for Ella Quinn and Riley.

I deflate a little. What's the point of having friends now if they aren't even around when I'm looking for them?

There's a bench in the yard where I usually sit in the mornings—everyone is usually too excited to see their friends and run around with them first thing in the morning to worry about the benches, so it's almost always free—and it's still empty because, as far as everyone else at school knows, I'm still that girl who doesn't have any friends and who writes in a notebook on the bench in the mornings. I don't know if everyone is leaving it for me or they pay so little attention to me that I just sort of slip out of the picture if I'm not around. I also don't know if I want to think too hard about that question, so I take my usual seat and then start tapping my fingers nervously against the wood.

Over the weekend I was pretty sure that Ella Quinn, Riley,

and I were really onto something. I told them what I thought about Tyler, how he's liked *so many* girls in the last year and how he clearly has no problem doing this to Ella Quinn, so why wouldn't he do it to all of them?

Ella Quinn had gone pale. "Oh my god," she said. "How long do you think he's been doing this? Do you think . . . Do you think it started with me? Like, he decided he hates me and now he does this to everyone?"

"I love you," Riley said. "But I don't think you're this guy's supervillain origin story. I think he just kind of sucks, and he's focusing all that he-sucks energy onto you right now, but he might have done it to other people before you."

"And he might do it to other people after me!" Ella Quinn had exploded. "So we need to figure out a way to make it stop *now*."

We couldn't decide exactly how we were supposed to do that over one night, but I thought that it meant we were working on it. I thought we were in on it together and we were going to try to take Tyler Harris down together. But now neither of them is anywhere to be found, and I start to feel a little itchy.

What if Ella Quinn and Riley think they made a mistake inviting me to sleep over? What if they realized that everyone is going to be super confused that Ella Quinn, of all people, is suddenly hanging out with *me?* What if Ella Quinn is worried that Tyler's going to tell more people that she's gay, so hanging out with me is too much of a risk? If you don't want people, or at least not twelve-year-olds, to think you're gay, the first step would probably be to stop hanging out with the gay girl.

I want to stand up on the bench and yell at everyone hanging out in their groups that I went to a sleepover at Ella Quinn's house over the weekend and there weren't any fashion shows, but we stayed up until three in the morning and it was way more fun than anyone in my class would think I'd have on the weekend.

But I'm not sure that would make it seem like I'm totally cool and fun to be around.

Instead, I sit on my bench and look around from behind my notebook, the same thing I do every morning. I look at the group of guys throwing a tennis ball against one of the school's walls even though they aren't supposed to because someone always tries to land one on the roof. I look at Jada Sumach and Jennifer Patel whispering intensely to each other like they always do. I look at the girls Ella Quinn is always nice to but isn't close with.

And then I look at Mr. Pitts stalking toward me so quickly he looks like a shark and I jump before I can stop myself. The morning sun is glinting off his bald spot menacingly.

"You're coming with me," he says, and I actually have to stop myself from laughing because he sounds like he should be speaking with an old-timey Southern accent. The Sheriff of Middle School.

Mr. Pitts jerks his head toward the school and people are starting to look over at us, but I put my head down and follow him inside. At first, I figure he somehow found out that Miss A let me out of detention early last week and he's going to make me sit in a classroom for twenty minutes because he can't let anything go, but then he steers us toward the office and a bit of color drains from my face.

Riley's sitting in one of the uncomfortable brown chairs in the reception area, and she gives me a grimace that I return. I know I should be more worried about sitting in the office—and I am, don't get me wrong! Kids like me aren't supposed to be called to the office before school even *starts*—but another part of me is just happy to realize that Ella Quinn and Riley weren't avoiding me. I didn't make the weekend up. They aren't regretting making a group chat with me.

"And how were you expecting me to find out this . . . this *campaign* against my son was occurring? Is *no one* doing their job here?"

It's a woman's voice, coming from the back offices where the principal sits.

Well, crap.

"Park yourself," Mr. Pitts says, and I hesitantly take a seat beside Riley before he stalks off.

"Do you think he gets a salary, or is he paid per head, like a bounty hunter?" Riley whispers, and I have to hide my laugh in my hands because Mr. Vickers, the terrible secretary who's never smiled in his life yet has a million framed pictures of a wiener dog at his desk, gives me a look.

"What happened?" I ask.

Riley rolls her eyes. "Ella and I got to school and Pitts was right there dragging us in here. I guess Tyler came home muddy the other day, but didn't want to talk about it. His mom finally got him to tell her what happened. Except Tyler told her this new version of it, where you pushed him too hard while you guys were playing tag on purpose, because of how he broke up with Ella Quinn."

"Why would *I* be the one to push him if that was the reason?"

Riley shrugs. "I don't know, but Tyler's mom is *pissed*. She's been calling the school all weekend to tell them they *abused* her precious son by letting him wear muddy pants without calling her, so now they have to tell us how terrible we are or I think she'll *actually* set up camp here."

"Is Ella Quinn going to tell them what Tyler's been doing?"

Riley makes a face. "What good would it do? She's tried before and Tyler didn't even get detention because he told Pitts that he was just joking and Ella didn't get it."

"Maybe Mrs. West will be different," I suggest. "She's a girl. Maybe she'll get it."

Riley takes a long, deep breath, and then shrugs. "It's never different, really."

Just as I'm about to tell her how depressing that thought is, Mrs. West comes out of her office.

"Both of you," she says, and then turns around in a way that makes me think that Riley may have a point.

16

Tyler's mom doesn't look the way I thought she would.

Everything I've ever heard about her made me think she'd be this weird, intense woman ready to squawk about how everything her son's ever done wrong is somehow someone else's fault. I pictured her with a messy bun and an expensive purse and maybe a monocle that she would use to peer at everyone she deems unfit for her baby boy. Or maybe she would look like the kind of person who eats babies and screams at anyone who gets in her way and won't stop until Tyler is President of the World. To be honest, I think I was picturing an in-character Meryl Streep.

But Mrs. Harris is wearing a suit and her dark hair is neatly styled and her makeup is nice. I thought she might be some kind of mess, like a soccer mom gone off the rails, but she looks like the type of person who's supposed to listen to reason. If you put her in a lineup and asked me to point at trustworthy people, I'd probably point to her.

Ella Quinn is sitting off to the side, two empty chairs squished between her and Tyler's mom like neither Mrs. Harris nor Ella Quinn could bear to be near each other. She doesn't look up at us when we come in, but I see her squeeze the edge of her seat until her knuckles go white.

She feels guilty, I think, surprising myself. I thought you had to be friends with someone for a really long time before you could understand what they were thinking, but I already know exactly what Ella Quinn's doing. Blaming herself for whatever's about to happen, even though it's *beyond* not her fault.

"I'm sure you understand why we're all here today, girls," Ms. West says to Riley and me.

"Because Tyler's harassing Ella Quinn?"

I ask it before I even realize I'm going to speak and Tyler's mom looks like her head is going to explode.

"I want her parents to be informed of this," she says to Mrs. West, who nods. It just makes me angrier, and I try to lift my head up even higher. Bullies raise bullies, I guess. If I was able to talk to Tyler in front of all his friends the other day, talking to his mom should be no problem.

"He's harassing her," I say again. "I have proof."

Mrs. West smiles apologetically at Tyler's mom. "I'll speak to them."

Tyler's mom gets up in a huff and turns to me. "You're very lucky I have to go to work. I *will* be calling your parents."

That doesn't scare me as much as I think she thinks it does.

Tyler's mom storms out of the room, which makes me wonder why we were brought in here to begin with.

"It's true," Riley says once she's gone. "Hazel was just trying to talk to him. To get him to leave Ella alone."

"I'm sure Ella can fight her own battles, girls," Mrs. West says. "In fact, Riley, you can leave. Mrs. Harris wanted you here, but . . ."

Mrs. West trails off because we all know that the end of that sentence is *but that makes no sense because this has nothing to do with you.*

Riley turns uneasily, giving Ella Quinn and me a look like *be careful.* I know what she's thinking, too. And I know that she'll be waiting for us outside the office. Mrs. West gives Riley a tight smile, like she's happy to get her out of her hair.

I've never liked Mrs. West. On our first day of middle school, she spoke at an assembly where she told us she wouldn't be calling us *kids,* but *young adults,* because we're all capable of making our own decisions now. She's spent pretty much all of our time here since then explaining how that's not actually true.

"Ella, I'm sure you know that saying things like that is a very big deal," Mrs. West continues. "That's a serious accusation."

Ella Quinn doesn't respond. She stares at the wall behind Mrs. West's shoulder.

"Tyler's mother wanted to have you girls suspended," Mrs. West says to Ella Quinn and me. "It took her all weekend to encourage Tyler to speak up about what you've been doing to him. She seems to think that the reason Hazel pushed Tyler last week was because you told her to, Ella."

Well, that's offensive.

Ella Quinn's eyes go huge.

"That's not fair!" she says. Her voice sounds thick, like she's going to cry. "He's the one who won't leave me alone. He's the one sending me horrible messages online."

"Is he?" Mrs. West asks, raising her eyebrows.

"Yes!" Ella Quinn says. She pulls her phone out of her pocket and brings up her I Wonder page. "Look. He's the one who should be suspended."

"He always spells the word *difficult* wrong," I add. "Look at one of the messages, it's spelled the way he always spells it, with an *e*, see?"

Mrs. West takes Ella Quinn's phone and scrolls through Tyler's messages. Her eyebrows get higher and higher.

"First of all," she says. "Miss Quinn, you know the rules. Your phone shouldn't be turned on during school. You can come get it at the end of the day."

She puts Ella Quinn's phone into a basket on her desk.

"The school day hasn't started yet!" I exclaim.

"Second of all." Mrs. West completely ignores me. "The trouble with your *proof* is that there's no shortage of spelling errors on the internet. Ella, do your parents know you have an account on this website?" Mrs. West asks.

Ella Quinn squirms and Mrs. West smiles at her. The kind of smile you'd give to a little kid learning how to ride a bike.

Mrs. West reaches into a drawer and pulls out a pamphlet. On the front, there's a picture of a blond girl with pigtails looking sad, her face lit up by the glow of a laptop. It says *Cyberbullying:*

Don't Be a Victim. I twist up my face at it and don't even care that it looks disrespectful to Mrs. West.

"You're too young for social media," Mrs. West says to Ella Quinn.

"She's too young to be getting messages like that, too," I say. "Shouldn't that be the focus here?"

"I'm sorry you've gotten some . . . hurtful messages, but that sort of thing happens on websites like I Wonder. I don't know why you assume they're from Tyler. That's the problem with the internet, ladies. You open yourself up to that sort of thing when you make yourself publicly available. And, on the internet, everything is publicly available, whether you think it is or not."

We're all silent for a moment. I can feel Ella Quinn shaking beside me and I want to try to help her calm down somehow, but I think I'm shaking too.

"I talked Tyler's mother down from the suspension. You'll have lunchtime detention for a week, Ella, starting tomorrow. *And* you'll write Tyler a letter of apology."

"She didn't *do* anything!" I say. "I was the one who was there when he fell. Ella Quinn wasn't anywhere near either of us. Even if Ella Quinn *did* tell me to do something, which she didn't, I was still the only one there. Why would she be punished over me?"

"Yes, well. I spoke to your homeroom teacher, Hazel," she says. "She's assured me you've never done anything like this before. I know it can seem tempting to do things to impress the cool kids, but it's never worth it."

"Are you telling me you don't think I'm *cool enough* to stand up for someone else?"

She ignores me again.

"Does that sound fair, Ella?"

Ella Quinn's quiet for a minute. I almost think she's not going to respond, but then she asks, "Are you a feminist, Mrs. West?"

Mrs. West looks surprised. "Yes, of course I am."

"Aren't feminists supposed to believe women with stuff like this?"

Mrs. West laughs like Ella Quinn caught her off guard. "I *do* believe women, thank you. But you aren't a *woman*, Miss Quinn. You're a little girl. Maybe you should act your age, and you wouldn't have to worry about things like this."

We leave the office in a daze, neither of us saying anything while I try not to pay attention to the way that Ella Quinn is sniffling. Once we get back into the lobby, though, I explode.

"Maybe you should *act your age?*"

Riley jumps up from where she's been waiting for us.

"She did *not* say that to you."

Ella Quinn walks out of the office ahead of Riley and me and we scurry behind her.

"She did," I say. Ella Quinn doesn't seem like she wants to talk about it, but she doesn't stop me as I explain everything that happened. By the time I'm done, Riley's mouth is hanging open like a fish. "You *open yourself* up *to that sort of thing?!*" she repeats, shocked.

I rub both my hands over my face. I can't believe that happened. I can't *believe* that happened.

"I can't believe that happened," Riley reads my mind.

The bell hasn't rung yet, so Ella Quinn leads the three of us back outside to the yard. She doesn't seem to know where we're going after that, so I take over and lead us to my bench. This is the first time I've ever sat on it with other people, unless you count that one time Kaden didn't see me and accidentally sat on my lap.

"It happened," Ella Quinn says once we're all squished together on the bench. She sounds a little dazed, like she can't quite believe it, but it definitely, definitely happened.

I've never understood the phrase *seeing red* until now. Everything about me is just *angry*. I feel it in my whole body. It makes me want to scream and break things and get right in Mrs. West's face until she *believes us*.

"That's not the first time, y'know?" Ella Quinn continues. "I don't think it'll be the last, either. Why would you believe Tyler over me?"

"You know why," Riley says. "Because he's a guy."

"And I'm just *a little girl*," Ella Quinn spits. "You'd think they'd want to protect such a helpless little girl."

Riley calls Mrs. West the *B*-word under her breath. Normally I wouldn't use that word, but if not now, when?

This is awful. Is this what happens when you have friends? Now I get sad when Ella Quinn is sad?

"We have to *do* something," Riley says.

"What are we supposed to do?" Ella Quinn snaps. "We tried

telling Pitts *and* Mrs. West what was happening and neither of them believed us. Do you think if we do that exact same thing again suddenly they're going to have a change of heart and totally flip positions?"

"So we won't do the exact same thing," I say.

Ella Quinn looks *exhausted*. Where Riley and I are angry, she's just worn down. It makes me even angrier.

"When you think about it, we know Tyler better than *anyone*," I continue. "Better than his friends, because he wouldn't *dream* of talking about his feelings with them. So we use that. I know every girl he's liked or dated in the last *year*. Trust me, there's a lot of them. Mrs. West can ignore three of us, but could she ignore thirty?"

Riley slowly nods. "She couldn't. She'd have to listen. If not to thirty girls, then at *least* to thirty parents."

"All we have to do is find them and hear them out," I say. "The way no one else seems to be doing."

The way I didn't, either. I don't think Ella Quinn is still mad at me for not believing her right away, but that doesn't mean I don't still feel bad about it. Why would I *ever* have believed Tyler over Ella Quinn? Just because he gave me little crumbs of attention? I don't even *want* attention from Tyler!

"We can do that," Riley says. She turns to Ella Quinn. "Ella, we can do that. We could hear them out."

I watch Ella Quinn weigh the options. It's almost as if I can see the pros and cons list she's making in her head. Of course she *wants* to take Tyler down. Of course she *wants* to help out all these hypothetical other girls. But the reality is closer to what just happened in the office. The reality is being called a little girl and getting in trouble, having your parents called and not knowing whether they'll believe you either.

"We only have to start with one," I tell her.

Ella Quinn thinks about it for another long beat. It almost looks like all the fight has gone out of her, her hair barely done, dark circles starting to form under her eyes.

But she's still Ella Quinn. She stands up tall and takes a deep breath and speaks with her chest the way you're supposed to when you give a speech and says, "We can do that."

17

We set up camp in the cafeteria—me, Riley, Ella Quinn, and her notebook opened up to a blank page titled *Operation 30* (the notebook is the exact same brand and color as mine, in nearly just as peak condition. I can't believe I spent so much time thinking Ella Quinn was my nemesis when she might in fact be my friendship soul mate). The three of us sit together at lunch to talk with our heads close together. I only think about the lice risk like one or two times, which I'm counting as a win. I'd thought that people would be wondering about what I was doing with Ella Quinn. I thought they'd be whispering to each other and asking each other why she'd ever hang out with me. But I don't think anyone notices at all. I'm invisible still, but this time it feels good. If no one cares what I'm doing, why should I care?

As usual, everyone else scarfed down their lunches as quickly as humanly possible. Now we have the whole table to ourselves. Ella Quinn provided the notebook, I provided the pencil case (after some debate over whose color-coordination system was more efficient), and Riley is providing a running commentary on how much she hates Mrs. West. She keeps getting so worked up that her words all blur together and her face scrunches up. I know it shouldn't, because this is Serious Business, but it makes me smile. All we have left to do is plan.

"So Tyler's been telling me about girls he likes since the beginning of the year, but he's told me about girls he used to like going back to last year, too," I say. "I'd guess most of the bigger crushes started just before winter break last year?"

Ella Quinn scoffs and writes *twelve months of nasty* in a neat bullet point. I realize what I just said.

"Sorry." I wince. There's a reason all of Tyler's crushes seemed to start just before winter break—that was just before he decided to break up with Ella Quinn.

"Don't apologize." She rolls her eyes. "Dodged a bullet. Or, at least, *trying* to dodge a bullet."

Riley knocks her shoulder against Ella Quinn's and Ella Quinn gives her a little smile. I realize I might be a tiny bit jealous, maybe, at the way they've always had someone to be there for them.

"I think we can probably divide the girls up into categories," I continue, shaking my head a little to remove any of the jealous thoughts. "I'd need a yearbook to remember all of them, but there were the ones he actually dated, and then the ones he liked."

"What's the difference?" Riley asks.

"The ones he liked but never dated either didn't want to date him, which, grossly, was rare, or they said or did something he didn't like and he decided they weren't worth his time."

"So there's our first group," Ella Quinn says. "He'd be mad at them, right? The same way he's mad at me now."

I haven't told Ella Quinn and Riley something.

When I got into class this morning, Tyler was waiting to corner me by our desks. Kaden was there too, either standing guard or just hanging around to see if I'd freak out and knock Tyler down again.

I tried to ignore them, but before I could turn away from Tyler he grabbed my wrist. Hard. Not hard enough to hurt, but hard enough to stop me in my tracks. To freak me out a little. To intimidate me for just a second.

"I hope you and your new girlfriends learned not to mess with me," he said in a low voice that he probably thought would scare me into submission.

"Yeah, we learned a valuable lesson," I said. I yanked my arm away from Tyler and just barely resisted the urge to turn the momentum into a slap. "We learned that you'll call your mommy to fight your battles whenever someone tells you no."

Kaden actually laughed at that. He looked at me like he was seeing me for the first time, and he was impressed. I was kind of impressed, too.

But Ella Quinn and Riley don't need to know that right now. I don't need Ella Quinn to feel guiltier than she already does.

"Yeah, he would've been mad," I say now.

"So we start there," Riley agrees. "We'll go where he's more likely to have done something. How many of those girls were there, Hazel?"

I try to think back on the last few months. As soon as Tyler started talking to me about his crushes, it was like he couldn't stop himself. Some days he's started by talking about one girl, only to have totally forgotten about her by the time lunch was over. On to the next one. If I'd known that I'd need to use all of Tyler's secrets in an elaborate plot to take him down one day, I probably would have listened a little harder.

"I'm not sure," I admit. "Like . . . a handful? Most of the time he either just asked them out and they said yes, or they'd do something he didn't like before it could even get to that point. I swear, a couple of times he'd go through more than one girl a day. I used to think it was because he was too afraid of liking someone who didn't like him back, but now I'm pretty sure it's just because he sucks and he has shockingly high standards for someone who sucks as much as he does."

Ella Quinn and Riley kind of deflate and I look around the cafeteria hoping that inspiration strikes. Unfortunately, it's still just a middle school cafeteria. I don't think very many people have ever been inspired by one. The same kids are napping on tables, the same kids are laughing in the corner. Maya Hutton is still reading by herself a few tables down from us.

"Maya Hutton!" I blurt out, and then cover my mouth. Thankfully, Maya doesn't seem to hear me.

"What about Maya Hutton?" Ella Quinn asks, trying to

peek at her over her shoulder without being obvious (it's obvious).

"Last year, just before summer," I explain. "Tyler had a crush on Maya for, like, the entire month of June, apparently, and wouldn't do anything about it. He *finally* asked her out, but she said her parents didn't let her date. Tyler was *pissed*. He kept talking about how she ruined his whole summer. If there's anyone he'd have been mad at, it's her."

For a second, we all peer at each other cautiously. It's one thing to decide we're going to approach all of these girls and try to get them to tell us the horrible things Tyler Harris did to them. It's entirely another to actually go and *do it*.

"Why am I so nervous?" Ella Quinn laughs at herself but I can see the way her hands are shaking.

"We don't have to do it if you don't want to," Riley says, and I nod along.

"I just . . ." Ella Quinn lets out a big breath. "What if he didn't do anything to her? What if he didn't do anything to *any-one*, and it's just *me*? Then it's like *what did I do* that made him act like that?"

"Nothing!" Riley and I say at the same time.

"It's *his* fault," Riley reminds her. "That's why we have to go all street justice and sneak around like this. I'm very busy, you know. I wouldn't do this if Tyler didn't deserve it."

"You *are* a very busy woman," Ella Quinn says with a tiny smile, and they both laugh.

We try to approach Maya cautiously, but it turns out it's hard to look nonthreatening when there are three of us and one of her.

She carefully puts her book down and looks around like we're going to try to Be Bad Influences on her.

"Hi," Ella Quinn says. "Can we talk to you for a second?"

Maya hesitates, so Riley adds, "Seriously, just for a second. Then can we talk about that book? I *still* haven't read it, so no spoilers!"

An *excellent* move by Riley. Maya smiles and we sit down beside her.

"So Tyler Harris asked you out last year, right?" Ella Quinn asks.

Maya goes pale. "I turned him down," she says. "If this is, like, a jealousy thing, I swear nothing's going on with me and Tyler. My parents are strict. I'm not even allowed to date."

"Oh my god *no.*" It all comes out of Ella Quinn in one long breath and she laughs. "I *promise* it's not a jealousy thing."

"Has Tyler ever . . . said anything to you?" I ask. Fun fact: it's really hard to just come right out and ask someone *so, have you been sexually harassed by this specific person?* "I heard that he was really upset when you turned him down. We just wanted to see if you were okay."

Maya's eyes go huge, and I know we have our answer.

"Look," Ella Quinn says. She holds up her phone, open to her I Wonder account and all of Tyler's messages. Maya brings both her hands up to her face and covers her nose and mouth. "Has he ever sent you anything like this?"

Maya pulls out her phone so quickly she's almost a blur. I

guess that's what happens when you're talking to someone who actually believes you.

It's more of the same on her I Wonder account. The messages from Tyler have mostly stopped, but Maya saved them all. *Do your parents know ur a slut?* And *u looked disgustin today* and *watch where ur going with that ass* and worse and worse and worse as Maya scrolls.

"I never told anyone," Maya says. "I didn't have any proof that it was him, but it started right after I turned him down. I'm so sorry. Maybe if I had he wouldn't have done it to you."

"Well," I say, "that's kind of the other half of why we're here. We *did* tell someone. They didn't believe us. So we're trying to see if Tyler did this to other girls. We figure they can't ignore all of us at once."

Maya's hand snaps back up and she locks her phone. She stuffs it deep down into her backpack and zips it shut for good measure.

"No," she says. "I told you, my parents are strict. I'm barely allowed the *phone*, let alone an I Wonder account. If I told them what happened, I'd have to tell them about the account, and then I won't have a phone again until I graduate high school. And that's *after* they'd ground me for a million years."

Ella Quinn, Riley, and I all look at each other for a minute. I'd been thinking about all the possible outcomes of this plan since we came up with it. We'd find other victims. We'd talk to other girls Tyler dated and they'd tell us he was always a perfect gentleman. We'd get expelled for trying to ruin perfect Tyler Harris's perfect reputation. But finding another victim that wasn't even *allowed* to talk about it didn't even occur to me.

"I'm sorry," Maya says. "I'm really, *really* sorry. But whatever you end up doing, *please* leave me out of it."

Maya gets up and walks out of the cafeteria, even though we were the ones who came to sit with her.

18

Moping takes up a lot of time.

I've been feeling particularly mopey since lunch. I guess it has something to do with the fact that the only person my age who I've spoken to regularly for the entirety of seventh grade so far is actually a horrible monster terrorizing a bunch of girls in my grade. And I've been encouraging him! I could have told him to shut up or to leave me alone. I could have asked Miss A for a different desk assignment. I could have done *something*, but I didn't, because deep down it felt good to have someone like Tyler Harris tell me all about his life.

Moping also makes you sluggish, I realize. My last class is gym (thankfully *not* with Mr. Pitts today) and I can barely run a lap. Now, don't think I'm usually some kind of super-impressive athlete, because I am *not*. But I can usually run one measly lap!

By the time everyone's changing out of their gym clothes, I get distracted by my own thoughts and realize that I'm the last one in the changing room. I check my phone—the bell rang five minutes ago, which means my bus is leaving in three minutes. I race to finish getting changed and then race even faster down the hall to grab everything I need from my locker. I basically dump its contents into my backpack and then run to the bus zone. Where was this springiness an hour ago?

I make it right up to Krystal's window just as she's starting to close the door. She makes a face at me to remind me that she doesn't like stragglers, but otherwise lets me on without complaint.

"Hazel!" Riley's voice calls. It's the strangest feeling. I can't remember the last time someone saved a seat for me on the bus.

"We thought you'd skipped town," Ella Quinn says from the seat across from Riley and me. I realize that they're sitting on the wheel, the way I used to. Away from everyone else.

Well, everyone except for Bella Blake. She's sitting with her body facing us, one arm over the empty seat in front of her and the other over the back of her and Ella Quinn's seat.

I don't usually talk to most people, but I *definitely* don't talk to Bella Blake. She's a different kind of beast altogether.

No, really. That's what they call her. Bella the Beast. She has it embroidered on her gym bag, which she's always carrying, because nothing's more important to Bella than volleyball. And nothing's more important to the volleyball team than keeping Bella in top form. At the team's last game, apparently an actual college scout came to watch her play. And she's *eleven*.

"So, turns out Maya's not as quiet as we thought she was," Ella Quinn says once the bus rolls out of the parking lot. I try to turn to hear her better, but Krystal has this thing about us putting our feet in the aisle.

At first I'm not sure what Ella Quinn is talking about, but when I figure it out I'm *positive* I must have gotten it wrong.

"Did Tyler do something?" I ask. I cut myself off before I can ask the whole question in my head, which was *Did Tyler do something to* you?! *To Bella the Beast?!*

"Oh yeah," Bella says. "Ohhhh yeah."

"We've just been talking about it," Ella Quinn says. "But I wanted to wait until you got here before Bella told us the whole story."

Bella's face is a little red, which is the most shocking part of all of this. More shocking than Ella Quinn and Riley saving me a seat on the bus. More shocking than Bella Blake talking to me at all. Bella the Beast isn't the kind of person to get easily embarrassed. She's the type of person to challenge Mr. Pitts to an arm-wrestling match and win. I hate that someone as useless as Tyler can make someone as cool and strong as Bella embarrassed.

"It was last year, after we'd won the volleyball championships," Bella says. "Normally nothing would bring me down on that kind of a day, y'know? It was supposed to be the best day ever. But then Tyler saw me in the hall—I guess he was at the game?—and he . . ."

"You don't have to tell us," Ella Quinn reminds her. "Seriously, if you don't want to talk about it you don't have to."

Bella shakes her head. "Ugh. No. It's just *embarrassing*. It's so *stupid!* Tyler saw me in the hall and said, *good game, Beast.* And, like, that's not normally a problem. Everyone says that to me after a game. I usually love it. But as he said it, he slapped me on the butt. Hard. Like it belonged to him. Like he thought he could do it whenever he wanted."

My heart drops straight to my feet. You can try to convince people that they've misunderstood Tyler when he says horrible things. Getting physical with someone who *clearly* doesn't want that is a lot more difficult to misunderstand or explain away, *Mrs. West.*

"I didn't want to go near him for weeks after," Bella continues. "I mean, I still don't want to. It's embarrassing all over again, every time I see him. It was ages ago, but I can't get it out of my head. Sometimes I catch myself rushing to lean against the wall when Tyler walks by, just so he doesn't have . . . y'know, access."

"Did you tell anyone when it happened?" Riley asks.

Bella grimaces and shakes her head.

"Sometimes the girls on the team talk about stuff like that," she says. "It doesn't seem like it bothers them when it happens. Some of them think it's funny. I guess I thought they wouldn't think it was a big deal."

None of us say anything until Bella continues. She says what we were all thinking.

"Plus, no one else was around, so it would be him against me. Pitts is *obsessed* with that kid. He'd win every time. I just . . . tried to get over it. But then Maya told me you guys asked her about the messages he sent her—"

"Has he sent you anything?" I leap forward and ask. Bella has an almost unlimited well of patience with the teachers. People love the school because of her. Maybe Mrs. West would listen to us with a superstar like Bella on our side.

But Bella just sighs and shakes her head.

"He never sent me anything," she says. "Maya said I should tell you guys about it, but I don't have any proof. Sorry."

"God, don't *apologize*." Ella Quinn almost laughs, which makes Bella laugh.

"He's barely spoken to me since," Bella says. "At first I thought it was because he felt bad about what he did, so I was starting to get used to the idea of forgiving him. In my head, at least. But now that I know what he's been doing . . . I think he just got worried he'd get caught after he did something so blatant."

It makes me want to slam my head against the gray plastic bus seat. Of course that's what he's doing. Tyler's basically just biding his time before the next butt to slap or girl to torment.

"Maya didn't say what you guys were doing with this," Bella says then. "But I wanted you to know that you're on the right track. Tyler sucks. And if you guys are bringing this to Mrs. West, I'll back you up. I just want to make sure that if we speak up, something actually happens to him."

None of us say anything to that. Of course that's what we want too, but we all know we can't guarantee anything. Not now that we've already tried.

Bella gets off at the first stop, so we don't have much more time to talk to her about any of this. She gives all of us a small smile before she leaves, and something feels different in my chest.

I'm not really sure what to do with it. It's half relief that someone else knows what's going on, half big, bad sadness because, *god*, someone *else* knows what's going on. I know I was the one who came up with the whole plan about finding all the other girls, but now that there definitely *are* other girls it's harder to deal with. What if we're digging up things that don't want to be dug up?

19

"So . . . now what?"

I ask it first thing the next morning, while we shiver together on my usual bench and wait for the bell to ring so we can go inside. I actually appreciate the way the three of us have to squeeze together to fit. Ella Quinn and Riley are surprisingly effective space heaters. Before, I just had to bundle up, cross my legs, and try and bunch them into my coat. This is a little easier. And kind of nice, but I wouldn't say that out loud.

I'm hoping that Ella Quinn or Riley will have some kind of plan, or at least an answer for me. But they both kind of sigh, and I can tell they feel just as defeated as the conversation with Bella yesterday made me feel.

"I know you're not supposed to say this when you're, like, fighting the good fight," Riley says. "But sometimes I wonder if this is worth it."

"It has to be worth it," Ella Quinn says. She still sounds tired, like this week has aged her (and it's only Tuesday), but at least now she's remembering that she's angry. Maybe the strength of our rage can power us through.

"If it's not worth it, that means we aren't worth it," Ella Quinn says. "And I can't just . . . keep living in a world where we aren't worth it."

My parents should take notes from Ella Quinn. She's not even *trying* to give a pep talk and I feel 100 percent more pepped up than I ever do from them.

"So let's figure out our plan, then," I say. "What have we been doing so far that we should be doing differently?"

"We've been trying to find girls that Tyler liked or dated," Riley says. "What other options do we have? It's not like we can find girls that he's *going to* like in the future."

Tyler has *a lot* of tells. I always thought that if I knew how to play poker and there was ever a way to get him into some kind of high-stakes game, I could clean up. If he likes a girl, he acts like he's the only person who's ever had a crush before. He stops answering questions in class, he gets more irritable with his friends, and he looks at me all sad until I finally ask him what's going on.

If he's dating a girl and it's going well, he doesn't speak to me. I don't think he speaks to anyone about it, really. Unless you count making gross jokes about the poor girl to Kaden. Once it's going badly (and it always goes badly, eventually), *then* he wants to talk. He groans and sighs and looks moodily out the window until I finally can't take it anymore. I don't even have to ask him what's wrong. The second I look at him it all starts coming out, how annoying or stupid or clingy she is and how hard it's going to be for him to dump her because he feels so bad for her. I always watch the girl after he's turned on her. They never see it coming, and then whenever Tyler does cut it off (he's stopped the public breakups since the Ella Quinn necklace incident), she always looks *so* sad. For about a day. And then she's with her friends and laughing and it doesn't seem like she even remembers what her life was like the week before.

Tyler clearly makes a lasting impression.

"Maybe we can't figure out who he's going to like next," I say, "but I bet we can figure out who he likes right now."

"What good would that do us?" Riley asks.

I snort. "Tyler likes to mope for at least a week before he does anything when he decides he *really* likes a girl. If he doesn't care so much, he'll move on in a few days. Or a few hours. But if he's *really* going for it, then there's a way to tell. If we can figure out who he likes right now, we'll have *plenty* of time to talk to the girl before he'd strike. Maybe we could get her on our side. She could be our spy."

Ella Quinn straightens up a bit.

"We could at least warn her before she gets involved in any of this," she says.

"Exactly!" I say.

I look around the yard. Tyler's always one of the easiest people to spot: find a big crowd, and he'll be right in the middle of it, wearing his neon yellow jacket that I guess is cool because a lot of the other guys started wearing them once Tyler got his.

The only problem with this plan is that Tyler's tastes are surprisingly wide-ranging. I guess he thinks he's high enough on the food chain that he can pretty much do whatever he wants without being questioned, so he'll go for anyone, from any friend group, as long as he thinks she might be up to his standards. It's not like we could just watch the group of girls that hangs out with the group of guys Tyler hangs out with.

"What if Tyler doesn't like anyone right now?" Riley asks.

I snort. "Yeah, that's not gonna happen. Tyler once told me he's actually *uncomfortable* when he doesn't like a girl. He said it just doesn't feel right. I think he needs projects. And these girls are his projects."

I add that last bit because I think Tyler's gross and I hate everything about him, but then I remember who I'm talking to and blush a little.

"No offense, Ella Quinn," I add.

She smiles sadly and waves me off, but I still feel bad.

It takes a whole day to figure out the next step of the plan.

Tyler isn't talking to me anymore, of course, so it's not as though I can just ask who his latest target is. In fact, he's started moving his desk ever so slightly farther away from me every day. Just an inch or so, so that Miss A won't notice for a while. But I notice everything. That's the point of me.

One of the things I notice on Wednesday morning, when Tyler sits down at his desk in a huff, so offended that we still share a last initial and he still has to sit beside me, is that his wrist is bare.

For as long as I've known Tyler, he's worn a blue rubber bracelet because his middle brother is a cancer survivor and his family did fundraisers for him when Tyler was little. He almost never takes it off. He even wore it during his swimming lessons last year (I don't know if Tyler didn't realize that I had swimming lessons at the same time he did, or if he's embarrassed that he's two levels below me, but he's never mentioned the fact that we used to see each other at the pool once a week).

But. Sometimes, when he's really trying to impress a girl, he lets her wear it. He tells her how special it is (even though Tyler's bracelet breaks all the time and his mom has a whole big bag of leftover bracelets, so he just replaces it right away) and lets her think that she's really special to him in trusting her with it.

If Tyler's not wearing that bracelet, some girl in this school is.

Which brings us here, to science, when Riley, Ella Quinn, and I are all sitting at our usual spots, all of us craning our necks to try to catch a glimpse of a girl wearing a blue rubber bracelet. Mrs. Haig hasn't come into class yet, so Ella Quinn and Riley can turn around in their seats and we can formulate our plan.

"Are you sure he didn't just forget to wear it today?" Riley asks. We're trying to whisper, because this is a top-secret mission, but it's pretty hard to do that in a classroom without a teacher, when everyone knows they can talk as loudly as they want.

"No," Ella Quinn and I say at the same time.

"He *never* takes that thing off," Ella Quinn says. "It fell off one recess last year and I had to spend the whole time trying to find it for him."

"He'd only take it off for a day," I continue. "To let a girl wear it. If he came home without it on, his mom would freak out on him. She always gets mad when she doesn't think he's treating it *respectfully*."

Suddenly, Riley's eyes go wide. She jerks her head to her right.

I glance in the direction she's motioning in and almost yelp out loud. We'd been so busy looking everywhere else in the room that none of us noticed that Brooklyn Caine has it proudly wrapped around her freckled wrist.

Brooklyn Caine is, also, sitting directly beside me.

For a second, the three of us just look at each other. What are you supposed to do in a situation like this? Did Brooklyn hear anything we just said? Do we just act like she didn't unless she tells us otherwise?

"Your hair looks nice today, Brooklyn," Ella Quinn chirps. Riley and I both jump at it and it kind of makes me happy to know that Riley's just as amazed at Ella Quinn's ability to turn on the charm at any given moment as I am.

Brooklyn touches her bright orange hair self-consciously. It's in a French braid, and I have to believe that it's at least a little because of Ella Quinn.

"Thanks," she says.

"Where have I seen that bracelet before?" Ella Quinn asks. She pretends to think about it.

She's good at a lot of things, but acting isn't one of them.

"Oh." Brooklyn goes bright red. When you're as pale as she is, that's *very* easy to do. "It's actually, uh, Tyler's? I told him I liked it and he let me hang on to it for the day."

Classic Tyler.

"Cool." Ella Quinn smiles and I watch Brooklyn try to figure her out. To understand why Tyler's ex would be so laid-back about some new girl wearing his bracelet. Relationships here last about two weeks, tops, but everyone remembers them for the next *century*.

Brooklyn goes back to pretending to go over her science notes—she doesn't have many friends in this class, which is how the two of us ended up sitting beside each other in the first place. It couldn't be a more perfect time to talk to her, since Tyler doesn't have science this period, and Brooklyn can't say that her friends are waiting for her, but Ella Quinn and Riley both look a little lost about how to proceed.

I take a deep, deep breath. I guess I'll have to channel my inner Ella Quinn.

"Actually, Brooklyn?" I say. "Could we talk to you about something really quickly?"

20

Brooklyn blinks at Ella Quinn's phone screen for a good long while before she speaks.

"That's horrible," she says. "But . . . you can't know for sure that it's Tyler who sent those, right?"

We gave Brooklyn our big speech, getting her up to speed on everything we know. Basically: Tyler sucks, we have proof, we want to make sure he can't keep doing this, do you want to help with that? Except, unlike when we spoke to Maya, we got to add a fun new line: for the love of all things good and pure in the world, please do *not* date this boy.

Brooklyn listened to us, which I consider a win in and of itself right now. Especially since I was the one to start the conversation. For the most part, I don't think of Oakridge as one of those schools where you can say something like *she doesn't even know my name*. It's a small enough school that it would be stupid to think something like that. But even though Brooklyn and I have been sitting beside each other all semester, I don't think she's ever spoken to me beyond asking to borrow a pencil.

"I used to talk to Tyler every day," I explain. "Do you see that typo in one of the questions? Diff-e-cult? That's how he spells it. I've had to tell him it's wrong before. And then when I tried to talk to him about it, he didn't deny it. He's almost proud of it."

"Still, though." Brooklyn chews on her bottom lip. "It's pretty hard to believe. No offense, Ella Quinn, but you aren't exactly the only girl Tyler's ever dated. Why isn't there some big, huge we-hate-Tyler club out there telling everyone how horrible he is? Why would he just do this to you?"

"He *has* done this to other people." Riley's starting to lose patience with Brooklyn and I reach my leg out to nudge her foot with mine. She jolts even though I barely touched her.

"Who?" Brooklyn leans forward.

I know we can't say Maya. She practically begged us not to bring her into this.

Bella didn't say anything like that. But all she really said was that if we were going to bring this to Mrs. West she'd have our backs. It's not as though she said *yeah, feel free to tell everyone about this incredibly embarrassing thing I've hidden from everyone I know for months.*

"We can't tell you," Ella Quinn says. "You'll just have to trust us."

Brooklyn nods, but not in an *okay, I trust you* kind of way.

Most of the other kids have gotten to class by now, and Mrs. Haig should be here any second. The four of us just sit there for a second, sizing each other up.

"Sorry I'm late, everyone," Mrs. Haig says, snapping all of us to attention. Everyone turns around and stops their conversations, and my heart sinks.

"Thanks for the warning, Ella Quinn," Brooklyn says, quietly, because Mrs. Haig is already talking about . . . Well, I don't know what she's talking about. Something sciencey, I think.

I know Ella Quinn and Riley have about ten seconds before Mrs. Haig yells at them for not facing the front of the room, but Ella Quinn looks so miserable about not being believed yet again.

"I'm sure it'll be fine," I say.

Ella Quinn tries to smile, but it doesn't really work. She and Riley turn around, and I watch Ella Quinn's shoulders slump.

I'm sure it'll be fine.

So y'know how whenever someone says *I'm sure it'll be fine* things are very rarely actually fine?

It happens at the end of the day, the three of us waiting in line for the bus. Miss A comes out of the school and scans the crowds of kids waiting. This weird feeling comes over me, one of those strange psychic moments you get sometimes. I know she's looking for me, and I know it isn't good.

Sure enough, Miss A spots me and starts making her way over. She's smiling, but it's not right.

"Hazel," she says, "Mrs. West has asked me to track you down. She just wants to speak to you in the office for a moment."

She's speaking quietly, probably so that no one overhears her and does that super annoying *ooooooh* thing kids do when someone gets called to the office. The problem is, though, that Miss A never comes out to the yard when we're getting on our buses, so everyone strains to hear her and then does the *oooooh* thing anyway.

Ella Quinn heard too, but that's because she'd been standing right beside me. She turns to Miss A and says, "Did she just say Hazel? Nothing about me? I think she probably meant me, too."

Miss A grimaces. "Sorry, Ella, just Hazel today. I'm sure she'll tell you all about it."

"What about the bus?" I ask.

"It shouldn't take very long," Miss A says. "They'll wait for you."

Oh, great. Now I get to be the last one on the bus after everyone knows I was in the office. So much for forgettable, quiet Hazel.

Before Monday, I'd never gone to the office alone unless I was running an errand for a teacher. I'm still not used to it. The halls seem longer, quieter, scarier when I'm actually being *sent to the office*.

Mr. Vickers clearly knew I was coming, because he barely looks up from his game of solitaire as he gestures for me to go through to Mrs. West's office. I'm expecting more of the same from last time I was in here: all hell breaking loose, essentially.

Instead, Mrs. West is smiling at me. She has a bowl of stale-looking jellybeans in front of her.

I've read enough fairy tales to know that it's a trap when a mean older lady offers you candy.

"Have a seat, Hazel," Mrs. West says. I almost want to ask *oh, you know my name?* She sure didn't seem to when she was blaming Ella Quinn for everything the last time I was here.

"I've been talking to your teachers," Mrs. West says. "It's funny, most of the time when there's a student in my office, I know exactly who they are. Do you know what I mean?"

"Sure."

"The . . . well, I wouldn't call them the *bad kids*, of course. But then, if kids like you are the good kids, what does that make them?"

Mrs. West winks at me. She *winks at me.* I decide it's best if I don't say anything. I'm a twelve-year-old girl: if there's one thing I know, it's how to tell when someone's acting friendly with you so that you'll start gossiping about someone else.

"But I didn't know who you were, the other day in my office," Mrs. West continues. "So I asked around, and I was absolutely amazed by the way your teachers never had anything but positive comments to say about you. They told me what a hard worker you are. They said you're always available to help other students. They said you were kind and courteous. Your homeroom teacher, especially, didn't think you were the type of girl who would get involved with any sort of bullying."

I feel a teeny pang of guilt. Miss A didn't need to stick her neck out for me like that.

"So, I started asking if anything had changed in your

situation." Mrs. West is clearly on a roll now. I'm not sure if she'd even realize if I left the room. Grownups love a monologue. "And can you guess what I found?"

I shrug.

"Your teachers mentioned that you've only just recently started socializing more with Ella Quinn. Is that fair to say?"

I shrug again. I feel like I'm in an old-timey cop show. Like she's about to shine a light in my face while I scream *I'm innocent, I tell ya, innocent!*

"Isn't she one of the good kids, too?" I ask. "She won the speech competition last year."

Mrs. West thinks about that for a second. "Well, not everything needs to be so black-and-white."

Everything was pretty black-and-white a second ago when you were telling me there were good kids and bad kids, I think.

"I always think it's great when I hear about students blossoming," Mrs. West continues. "That's what middle school is for, right? It's almost always a great idea to make new friends."

Neither of us says anything for a minute.

"But?" I prompt.

Mrs. West smiles tightly. "But sometimes those new friends can . . . influence us to do things we wouldn't otherwise do. And when that happens, it's not your fault!"

"Am I in trouble?" I ask.

Mrs. West shakes her head. "Of course not! I just wanted to talk to you. A couple of students have told me they're a little worried about Ella Quinn spreading rumors about Tyler Harris. I know we may have gotten off on the wrong foot about this before, but I want you to know that if you wanted to talk about any of this, my door is always open."

I ponder that for a second. I think Mrs. West thinks that means she's winning, because her smile gets even wider and more fake-nice.

"Who's been so *concerned?*" I ask. "Was it Brooklyn?"

"I'm sure you understand that I can't tell you that." Mrs. West's smile goes tight around the edges again.

I've learned a few valuable lessons over the last week or so. One of them has been to know when to swallow my anger down hard, even when it feels like it's going to burn through my skin, burn a hole through Mrs. West's office walls. Because there's a very specific reason why she called me down here and not Riley. Because she sees me as the weak one. The one she can be nice to and give jellybeans to and I'll immediately switch sides and tell her everything she wants to hear. She'd rather persuade me to change my mind than hear us out about Tyler.

"I'm not in trouble, right?" I ask again. My voice is raspy because I'm trying not to scream.

"Of course not, Hazel!" Mrs. West says.

"Okay," I say. "In that case, I don't have anything else to say."

I get up, and Mrs. West doesn't try to stop me.

All the other buses have left by the time I get back outside. Miss A is waiting beside my bus, and I breathe out a little sigh of relief when I see her. Krystal is usually a little less impatient when there's another adult around.

"Are you okay?" Miss A asks when she sees me.

"I'm fine," I mutter, and trudge onto the bus. Krystal doesn't even wait until I'm fully up the stairs before she closes the door behind me and starts driving. She must live a very rich life outside of being a bus driver, because she always seems very excited to get back to it.

Ella Quinn and Riley are waiting for me by our new usual spot, over the tire. When they see me they squish close together and pat the little spot beside them. We aren't usually allowed to sit three to a seat, but Krystal is too preoccupied with zooming around town to notice today.

"What happened?" Riley asks, and it all explodes out of me.

I launch right into everything: every word Mrs. West said and every word I should have said but didn't.

"Okay," Riley says slowly once I'm done—I'm actually breathing heavily after my monologue. "The fact that you didn't come on here screaming is extremely impressive."

"I'm so sorry," Ella Quinn says. She looks like she's about to cry and I panic. I might not be as bad at having friends as I thought I'd be, but I'm not sure I know how to deal with a crying friend yet. That feels advanced.

"It's not your fault!" I tell her for what feels like the billionth time. Ella Quinn deflates, dropping her head onto Riley's shoulder. For two bus stops, none of us says anything.

"Do you guys want to sleep over at my house on Friday night?" I ask.

Where the heck did *that* come from?

I go to one sleepover and now I think that solves all friend-related problems?

But Ella Quinn responds immediately. "Yes please," she says. "I have to have *some* kind of fun this week, or I'll turn to dust."

"It's good to see you're still being reasonable in the face of all this," Riley says, and Ella Quinn laughs, really laughs, for what feels like the first time since all of this started.

Riley turns to me next. "My parents are taking me to my grandma's this weekend," she says. "But you should go ahead without me! Send me pictures and call me if you need to bail Ella out of jail for egging Tyler's house."

"That won't be a problem," I say. "We'll be TPing it."

21

"My mom likes you,"

It's the first thing Ella Quinn says when I open the door on Friday night. She has her pink backpack over one shoulder and her mom waves out the window of her silver minivan at me before driving off. If I think about this too much I'll just be confused— how on *earth* have I gone from thinking Ella Quinn was my nemesis to being happy to see her when she's dropped off at my front door for a *sleepover* all in the span of, like, a week?

"I had to really convince her that I still deserved to do something fun this weekend even though I landed myself in detention all week, making me, of course, a horrible delinquent destined for juvie and god knows what else," Ella Quinn continues, rolling her eyes. "But she thinks you're a good influence, so here I am. Wow me."

I must make a face at that, because Ella Quinn laughs.

"Oh my god, Hazel, I'm joking," she says. "Consider me pre-wowed. I'm just happy to have something to do this weekend that doesn't involve sitting in my room alternating between practicing my speech and angry-crying about what Tyler's doing."

The rest of the week has been weird. Tyler left us alone, but it didn't feel like we won. He sat in the corner of homeroom and glared at me every chance he got, or worse, he'd huddle up with Kaden and every so often Kaden would shoot me a look. I think it was supposed to be intimidating?

It's not like we made them leave us alone, though. It feels like they're just waiting to come back even worse than before.

It was also the first time I actually felt like I didn't have any friends in homeroom. At the beginning of the year, when we got our class assignments, it felt like everyone but me was freaking out about not having the same one as their friends. I remember rolling my eyes at all of them — imagine being *upset* that you got Miss A over Mr. Pitts, chair-thrower extraordinaire? I thought they were being so dramatic, but now I think I kind of get it. When Tyler Harris is staring at you like he's thinking of a million ways to ruin your life, it would be nice to feel like you have a friend around. Or at least someone to remind you that Tyler Harris can't actually ruin anyone's life.

"Ella Quinn!" My dad comes up behind me even though he *promised* he'd stay in the kitchen until I brought her in myself. You have to ease people in with my parents. At least, I think you do. It seemed like a good idea when we had our pre-sleepover family meeting. "The great Ella Quinn! Hello!"

Ella Quinn laughs. "You can just call me Ella."

I blush. *Everyone* calls Ella Quinn Ella Quinn. I mean,

Riley doesn't, but that's different, right? They're best friends. It's not weird to keep full-naming her.

Except now I'm doubting myself. Does Ella Quinn—Ella—think I'm being too weird and formal for still calling her Ella Quinn? And if she does, how am I supposed to just *switch* to calling her Ella? Wouldn't that be even weirder?

It's possible I'm overthinking this.

"Well, welcome, Just Ella," my dad says.

Why is he *like this?* I barely resist clawing my fingers down my face.

"We're gonna go upstairs," I say before he can keep talking to Ella Quinn (or worse, start asking her *questions*). I dart out of the way and head upstairs without checking to see if she's following, but thankfully by the time I get to my room she's still there.

"Your dad seems nice," she says.

"He is," I agree. "He's weird, but, y'know . . . not so bad."

"Score!" My dad's voice comes from downstairs, where I guess he's *standing around listening to us* like an absolute *creep*, oh my *god*.

I open my bedroom door and all but shove Ella Quinn inside. The sooner we get away from him, the better.

My room is a lot smaller than Ella Quinn's. When my mom told me she was having Rowan, I got too excited at the idea of finally not being a weird only child and I said he could have my room. It was a moment of great weakness.

Now, Rowan has my old room. We painted his walls pale yellow and never got around to painting *my* room, so it's too white and it still doesn't feel like mine after almost a year. It's more like a hotel, or a room you stay in when you visit your cousins. My dad took me to Target and we got new bedding at least, bright blue with white polka dots. He said he'd put up bookshelves, but he hasn't gotten around to doing that either, so my books are in stacks dotted around the room. Every so often one of them falls over in the night and I have a heart attack.

It's not a sustainable system.

"It's super comfy in here," Ella Quinn says after she takes a look around.

I know that usually when people say things like *it's cozy!* they really mean that it's small, but that's not what Ella Quinn means, I don't think. She takes a seat on my bed and then says, "Ooh, this is so soft, where'd you get it?" And somehow it feels like she belongs here.

I don't know if everything I understand about sleepovers is flawed, or if Ella Quinn and I are just boring, but tonight, it's eleven thirty when we're both fading and Ella gets herself comfortable in a blanket nest on the floor beside my bed. I wasn't sure if I was supposed to offer my bed, but it's a little squishy even for just me, and I know Ella Quinn hasn't said anything mean about me liking girls (and I don't think she would), but there's probably a difference between her not saying anything mean and her being comfortable getting right up close and personal with me.

Or maybe not. Before we decided to go to sleep, she was pretty sprawled out on the bed with me while we watched Netflix on my old laptop. Her whole leg was hanging over my hips and the edge of the bed. So maybe that's another thing I'm worried about that I don't need to be worried about.

I fall asleep quickly. I've been going to bed earlier this last week. Ella Quinn looked really tired, too. I wonder if she feels the same way I do right now, exhausted all the time and waiting for the next thing to happen. The next detention, the next attack. My guard's been up 100 percent of the time. I think bedtime's been the highlight of my day all week.

Just as I start a very satisfying dream in which Tyler is being turned into a giant chicken, though, Rowan starts crying.

Rowan cries a lot, and I knew he would cry a lot when my parents brought him home. That's what babies do. I get that! No one ever told me that he'd be super quiet and calm the whole time. I'm old enough to understand the deal with babies. Normally I can sleep through it, anyway. He cries for a bit, my parents calm him down, we all go back to bed. It's not nearly as bad now that he's almost one as it was when he first came home.

Sometimes, though, Rowan *will not* calm down. I don't know what happens or what my parents try to do or what the problem is, but he'll start screaming and he won't stop until he decides to stop. Which could be in an hour, or three days.

As soon as I hear Rowan crying, I know it's one of those times. It's a particular screech that I've gotten very good at recognizing. Like if someone threw a cat at a wall and the cat fought back. I roll over and try to stuff my head under my pillow, praying that Ella Quinn is a heavy sleeper and she won't even notice.

Rowan cries on and off for an hour, and I lie there pretending like I'm asleep, trying to listen to see if Ella Quinn is awake. I can hear my parents shushing Rowan, singing to him, trying to do whatever they can to get him to shut up. I know it's not their fault but, also, they made him. So it kind of is, and I'll be blaming them for it.

By the time it's almost one in the morning and Rowan still hasn't stopped, I hear Ella Quinn roll over in her blanket nest.

"This might be a stupid question," I say into the darkness, "but are you awake?"

Ella Quinn starts laughing, which makes me laugh, and then we're both lying there laughing while Rowan's crying gets louder and louder and louder.

"I only have older sisters," she says. "I think I need to apologize to them now. *This* is what I put them through when I was a baby?"

"I'm sorry," I say.

"It's not your fault!" she says. "Does this happen every night? How are you still so good at school?"

I grin. Ella Quinn might not be my nemesis anymore, but it still feels good to hear her say I'm good in school.

"Not every night," I say. "Usually he goes right back to sleep. Sometimes, though . . ."

"What do you do when he gets like this?"

A slow smile creeps across my face.

"Do you like pancakes?"

22

I realized when Rowan was two months old that it's way harder to hear him cry from the kitchen. The kitchen's downstairs at the way back of the house and Rowan's room is upstairs at the front. It's the farthest possible point away from the screaming. It's not *perfect*—you can still hear him if you really focus. But it's definitely better than being just down the hall from him, when it feels like he's making the walls shake with his freakishly strong baby lungs.

My parents have found me asleep at the kitchen table in the morning, syrup in my hair and whipped cream melted in a puddle by my feet more than once. They let it slide because I think they understand that it's *basically* their fault, too.

There's not much to do in a kitchen alone in the middle of the night. It wasn't like I could text my friends. I had, like, three people in my contacts before this week. One of them was my grandpa. So one night I thought I might as well try to do what you're supposed to do in a kitchen.

As it happens, I've also learned that pancakes, which are one of the only things I know how to make by myself, taste better in the middle of the night.

I find an unopened package of chocolate chips in my mom's snack stash that she thinks I don't know about and dump half of it into the batter. I'm sure she'll forgive me, since it's *her* baby keeping us awake, and she actually cried when I asked if Ella Quinn could sleep over. We're making a huge mess, but we'll clean it up, and anyway, my parents were the ones so obsessed with me having friends. This is also their fault, really.

"I think we have . . . yes!" I say, digging in the fridge until I find a bottle of whipped cream. I check the expiration date and learn that it takes a *long* time for whipped cream to expire. That should maybe worry me more than it does. "Open, please."

Ella Quinn opens her mouth and I squirt whipped cream into it until it overflows. She snaps her head back to try to stop it from falling out, but it just ends up splatting onto the floor and Ella Quinn laughs so hard she snorts. She helps herself to a paper towel and cleans up after herself, and I can practically hear my parents swooning from upstairs.

This isn't my first pancake rodeo, so they all come out pretty well, if I do say so myself (we don't need to talk about the first burnt one. The first pancake doesn't count; everyone knows that). Ella Quinn offers to help, so I pass her the bowl and she proceeds to burn three pancakes in a row.

"I thought it would be easier than it actually is," she laughs.

Something about that is weirdly shocking to me. I think if I was at Ella Quinn's house and I burned a bunch of pancakes,

I'd spend at least a week beating myself up for it. I'd think I was stupid and I'd think that Ella Quinn was laughing at me. But I don't think she's stupid, and I don't want to laugh at her.

It's possible the main difference between Ella Quinn and me is confidence, but let's not dwell on that.

Ella Quinn and I sit down at the kitchen table and dig in. I'm not even that hungry, but something about it being the middle of the night makes it more fun. Thanks to all my Rowan-sponsored ice cream parties lately, we are *not* lacking for toppings. I found chocolate and caramel sauces, mini marshmallows, extra chocolate chips, and chocolate spread. Ella Quinn went wild and threw everything I put in front of her onto her pancakes. It's more chocolate than pancake (the ideal ratio). Before I even realize it, I'm tearing through pancakes like it's my job.

"Thanks for inviting me over," Ella Quinn says through her own mouthful, looking down at her plate.

"Thanks for not hating me when my brother basically screamed in your ear for an hour."

She laughs a little bit, but then her face starts to cloud over. Her lip wobbles, and I just have enough time to think *oh god, is she going to start crying? What do I do with that?* before the first tear falls down her cheek.

I wish Riley were here. Riley knows how to have a friend. She understands Ella Quinn. She'd know exactly what to say and how to make things better. I haven't reached that level of friend yet, I don't think.

"Are you okay?" I ask, which is stupid, because she's *crying*

at my kitchen table at two in the morning and she just sniffled and I'm
pretty sure chocolate sauce came out of her nose.

Ella Quinn nods and wipes her eyes.

"Sorry," she says. "It's . . . been a long week."

It really has been. And it's one thing for me to say that, but
entirely another for Ella Quinn. I've just been along for the ride,
really. She's the one who has to live with all of it.

"It just sucks," she says. Her eyes start to water again. "Why
don't they ever *listen?*"

Honestly, I don't know why she isn't angrier. I don't know
how she hasn't been crying like this all week. I don't know why
she hasn't been shoving Tyler into mud puddles all week—all
year. My fork feels heavy in my hand all of a sudden. Realizing
that not all grownups care—*really* realizing it, understanding it
like I guess I didn't before—is a lot for a Friday night. (Saturday
morning, technically).

"We'll make them listen," I say. "There has to be some way
to make them listen."

"How? Seriously. It's great to say stuff like that, but if they
see what's going on, if I tell them to their faces what's happening,
and they still don't do anything, what comes next?"

I don't have anything to say to that.

"It's not even that they aren't listening," Ella Quinn says
down at what's left of her pancakes. "It's that they are, but they
just don't care."

"Screw that!" I explode. Ella Quinn and I both pause to
make sure my parents didn't hear. When it seems like we're good,

I continue. "I don't care if they don't care. *I* care. Riley cares. If no adult is going to help us, we'll help ourselves."

Ella Quinn starts to smile. Only a little bit, but I think it still counts.

"This is why you're my toughest competition."

I laugh. "I am?"

"Yes! I was *so* sure you were going to beat me at the speech competition last year. My mom told me to write my speech on the tooth fairy but then yours was so funny, I thought there was no *way* I'd win. Honestly, I still don't know how it happened."

"Hyperbole," I mutter.

"What?"

My face is bright red. I know Ella Quinn isn't my nemesis anymore, but that doesn't make it any less embarrassing to acknowledge last year's fatal mistake. "That's why you won. I pronounced the word *hyperbole* like *hyper-bowl.*"

"You did? I don't remember that. Are you sure?"

"You didn't *notice?*"

"I don't think I even know what hyperbole means."

When it happened, I couldn't stop thinking about the judges and the other competitors and Ella Quinn laughing at me for getting it wrong. I could just imagine the judges congratulating Ella Quinn and telling her *it was close there for a second, but then Hazel Hill just handed you the win!* I was so sure that people would be talking about it for ages, saying things like *why did she think she could win a speech contest? She can't even pronounce* hyperbole*!* And I thought—I *knew*—that Ella Quinn would have been laughing along with them, because *she* would never do something that stupid. *She* must know how to pronounce *hyperbole*.

"What?" Ella Quinn asks. I realize I've been staring off into space thinking about something that happened last year for a bit too long for a normal conversation.

The thing is, even if Ella Quinn is lying to me, she's doing it to spare my feelings. I don't think she *is* lying, but now I know that she doesn't care if I mess up a word. She just wants to compete in the speech contest like I do and she wants to win it as much as I do.

But if we're friends now, how am I supposed to ruthlessly beat her at the speech contest and then laugh as she cries in defeat? Because that was the plan up until about two weeks ago, but now that seems really . . . mean.

"Have you been practicing a lot?" I ask. "For this year, I mean."

Ella Quinn grimaces. "Not as much as I should be. Every time I try, I just start going through these different scenarios and it turns into me yelling at Tyler. They aren't exactly prize-winning speeches. Or school appropriate."

"What . . ." I trail off. "This going to sound like a stupid question, but what happens if one of us wins?"

Ella Quinn cocks her head. "Then she gets gloating power for the rest of the year until the *next* speech contest, I guess? Maybe we go to the grocery store and buy a sheet cake and eat it all in one sitting in celebration? I hadn't given the end result very much thought, honestly."

Even I know that it would be a little corny to outright *ask* Ella Quinn if we'd still be friends if I beat her this year. But when I think about it, I'd still like to be friends with Ella Quinn if she beat me. And she's already done that, anyway, and she's friends with me now.

I didn't realize how much of friendship involved trying to solve very complicated problems in your head in the middle of a conversation without making it seem like that's what you're doing. This particular topic was not covered in health class discussions about healthy friendships.

"What are you thinking about?" Ella Quinn asks.

"Nothing." I smile. "Just trying to figure out how we can get Tyler to shut up."

It's a bit of a cheap shot to bring up Tyler again so that the focus leaves me, but desperate times call for cheap shots.

"Pushing him into the dirt didn't help," Ella says, sighing. "Like, you literally pushed him into the dirt! And that didn't even do anything!"

An idea starts to form in the back of my head.

"So maybe we need to . . . push him into the dirt."

Ella Quinn tilts her head at me.

"What did *I* just say?"

"No, not literally! Listen, Tyler sucks, right? He's mean and . . . and sneaky! So maybe we need to fight dirty! Maybe we need to be just as sneaky as Tyler is!"

Ella Quinn thinks about it for a long time. She stares down

at her pancakes, which have gone mushy now, and stirs them around a little.

Eventually, though, she looks up at me. She doesn't look like she's going to cry anymore. She's smiling, and it finally looks like she means it.

We get to work.

23

"Okay, can you explain the plan one more time?"

Ella Quinn and I groan. Riley's asked us to explain our plan to her at least three times. It's starting to feel more like she just doesn't like the plan. Which would be ridiculous, because our plan is foolproof and amazing. Ella Quinn and I stayed up all night on Friday and worked through most of the day on Saturday making sure it was perfect from all angles. Ella Quinn and I are two of the smartest girls in the seventh grade! Obviously any plan the two of us come up with would be unbeatable. And this plan is finally, *finally* going to prove once and for all that Tyler's the bad guy here.

"Hazel's going to try to talk to Tyler during homeroom this morning," Ella Quinn starts.

"He hates me right now," I admit. "But he's always so desperate to talk about his problems with me, and I bet he's not talking about any of them right now. I don't think it'll take very much convincing for him to start yammering on about girls or his mom or whatever."

"Exactly," Ella Quinn continues. "We're just trying to get him comfortable, so he doesn't see phase *two* of the plan coming."

"And phase two is . . . ?" Riley asks. Ella Quinn and I groan again.

"Phase two is when Hazel tries to talk to him at *lunch*," Ella Quinn reminds her.

"He's always talking about all the stupid stuff he's doing. He loves bragging about how amazing he thinks he is. I'll ask him about what's been going on and before long he won't be able to resist talking about the messages he's sending to Ella Quinn and what he did to Bella. He was *so* ready to tell me all about it the last time I talked to him."

"But the last time you talked to him it . . . didn't go so well," Riley points out.

"Well, no. *But!* This time, I'll have my phone in my hoodie pocket and I'll record him talking about it."

"We'll take that to Mrs. West and then there's no way she won't believe us!" Ella Quinn finishes.

I feel like I should bow or something. It really is the perfect plan. I finally feel like the spy Ella Quinn and Riley thought I was before. But now Riley furrows her brow and shifts her weight uneasily from foot to foot instead of applauding us.

"Why are you doubting the plan?" Ella Quinn asks her.

"I'm just worried about you guys," Riley says. Her hair's down today, which is unusual, and she tucks it behind her ear when she sees me noticing it. "I don't want you to get in any more trouble than you already have. Maybe it's less about getting Tyler in trouble at school, and more about getting him to stop with Ella. Isn't that what's more important?"

I want to be upset at that, but I know Riley just wants us to be okay. Ella Quinn and I came marching into school ready to tell her all about the plan this morning. In hindsight, we probably brought a lot of ready-to-fight-Tyler-Harris energy to a conversation that was happening before eight a.m.

"Let's just see what Tyler's like this morning," I say. It's weird being the middle ground between two people. I didn't think I knew how to have friends and now I'm suddenly an expert in keeping two of them? "If he's all . . . wired and creepy like he was last week, then we can think about a different plan. But if he's calmed down a bit, maybe it'll work, right?"

Riley tucks her hair behind her other ear.

"I saw Brooklyn over the weekend," she says.

Ella Quinn's eyes bug out of her head, and I'm sure I look just as shocked.

"You saw Brooklyn?" I ask. "Like, you guys hung out?"

"Ew, no." Riley wrinkles her nose. "We were grocery shopping and I saw her in the store. Our parents know each other from something, so they were chatting and Brooklyn started talking to me. It just left a weird taste in my mouth, is all."

"What did she say?" Ella Quinn asks.

"She's just kind of . . . she's girl-sneaky, y'know?" Riley says. "I know we're not supposed to say that, but that's the best way to describe it. She started talking to me like we were best friends all of a sudden and then she brought up Tyler. She was like, *hey, I hope everything's okay with Ella Quinn. I'm worried about her. What would have to be wrong with a person to make up all that stuff about Tyler?*"

"What would be wrong with a person to ignore *actual* sexual harassment?!" Ella Quinn explodes.

"I know," Riley says. "But I think that proves that she was the one who went to West. Not that there was ever much doubt of that. When I told her that you weren't making it up, she rolled her eyes at me and said something about how *there are two sides to every story* and went back to her parents. I'm just saying that if Tyler can get people on his side that easily, we should be more careful about how we do this."

Sure, it's not *awesome* that Brooklyn was swayed over to Tyler's side so easily, but I have to keep reminding myself that this isn't about sides. It's not like Tyler sent Ella Quinn a compliment that she misunderstood and now there's, like, *drama*. It's bigger than that.

"I'm always careful," I say, even though that's not strictly true. "Someone has to do something about it, and I think it should be me."

If I think about it too hard, maybe the whole reason I want Tyler to get in trouble so badly is because I feel guilty. Why didn't I stop him when he was talking about Ella Quinn so horribly? Why was I so ready to believe everything he said about her? I should have gone straight to Ella Quinn and told her what he was saying. Maybe if we caught it sooner, Tyler wouldn't have gotten this confident. Maybe I could have stopped it before it even got to this point.

Riley's giving me a funny look. Her hair's fallen into her face again, and she tucks it behind both of her ears at once this time.

"You know it's not your fault, right?" she asks me. "Tyler's always been the worst, but it's not your fault that he wasn't like that with you. He was always going to be like this, because no one's ever told him *not* to. But it wasn't your job to tell him that."

I don't really know what comes over me then. I see girls hugging their friends all the time at school—giving each other piggybacks, squeezing hands, and touching each other without even thinking about it. It always seemed weird to me. It felt like something that wasn't for me. Or I thought that if I tried it, people wouldn't like it. They'd misunderstand, even though I'd never given them anything to misunderstand. I thought if I ever tried to do something affectionate like that, I'd just look stupid, but I don't even think about stepping in closer and hugging Riley now. At first, she freezes, and I spend a horrible second thinking that all of those fears are coming true and this was a terrible idea. But then she squeezes me back, just a little, and it feels way better. It feels normal.

"Thanks," I say once we break apart. "You kind of just read my mind."

"I'll just be standing over here, then," Ella Quinn says. "You two enjoy your moment, it's fine! I'll be just fine here, all alone, by myself. Alone. Unloved. Unhugged."

Riley rolls her eyes at her, but she's smiling. She yanks Ella Quinn over by the arm and that's how I participate in my first multiperson hug since, I think, kindergarten.

"And"—I start digging in my jacket pocket until I find a hair elastic and I pass it over to Riley—"here. Not that your hair doesn't look nice down! It does. But you seem uncomfortable, and you shouldn't be. Not on *plan day*."

Riley ducks her head and thanks me. Both of us ignore the look Ella Quinn gives us. Like she's trying to figure something out, or like she already has and she's starting to take notes on the situation.

24

Tyler does this funny thing.

He could be completely in love with a girl on Monday morning, and then by lunchtime on Tuesday he's forgotten all about her. He's been so mad at his friends that it seemed like he was ready to fight them in the park after school, but then by the time the end of the day rolls around he's laughing and joking with them like nothing ever happened. Feelings don't tend to stick with Tyler. Not the small ones, anyway. He feels them hard for an hour or two, and then they melt away. His big feelings come out in a big way. Moping in class, complaining to me, icing out his friends for days at a time. Unfortunately, it seems like I've unleashed some of Tyler's Big Feelings just when I actually *want* him to talk to me like he used to.

When I walk into homeroom that morning, Tyler's already there. He's sitting at his desk, but he's turned in his chair so he's fully facing my seat beside him. He's even moved his desk back to where it used to be, in line with everyone else in his row and closer to me. (Thank goodness—that uneven row was starting to make my eye twitch.) It stops me in my tracks. For a second, I think he's figured out our plan and he's going to call me out on it right here. But then I remember that he's not smarter than me, he's just luckier. I know my job right now is to figure out what's going on with him, so I have to be normal, but all I want to do is kick his chair out from under him. Miss A hasn't shown up yet, so everyone's running around and yelling and telling each other what they did over the weekend. I feel a little smug: I *also* actually did something this weekend.

I sit down and pretend he's not staring at me.

"You know it doesn't matter that Brooklyn won't go out with me now," he says.

I arch an eyebrow at that. Brooklyn's seemed to be pretty pro-Tyler up until this point.

"I don't know what you're talking about," I say.

I wince internally. Only people who *do* know what someone is talking about say stuff like that.

Tyler scoffs. "Yeah, all right. I just wanted you to know that you actually saved me. She's *so* clingy it's actually insane. When I texted her, she would text me, like, four times in a row. Who *does* that?"

"So glad I could save you from the horrors of a conversation with a girl who somehow actually likes you," I say.

It's weird how easily I fall back into our routine. It's like nothing ever happened between us. Tyler doesn't bring up anything that's happened the last two weeks—the harassment, the push, what Ella Quinn said about having a crush on me. I know that if I don't bring anything up either, we could just go on like this.

It makes me angry. He's just like Mrs. West, I realize. He thinks I'm the weakest link and that he can make me love him by being a bit nicer to me than usual.

Too many people have thought too little of me lately.

"How was your weekend?" I ask in my Very Polite voice. And then I remember that I never start conversations with Tyler and panic a little.

(Internally, of course. Tyler's already thrown the plan off by talking to me right away. I need to stick to the actual plan as close as possible if it's still going to work.)

Thankfully (and predictably) though, he doesn't seem to notice or care about what I said. Instead, he lets out a long groan and rolls his eyes into the back of his head. He still makes sure to do it quietly, though. Can't have anyone realize that he's actually *speaking* to me. I ball up my hand into a fist underneath my desk and squeeze until I feel little crescent-shaped indents on my palm.

"Horrible," he says. "Have you ever liked someone so much that it feels like you're gonna throw up?"

"No."

"Right, I forgot you're, like, a robot. Anyway, Rebecca—"

"Rebecca?"

"Yeah. She's in eighth grade."

"So you just . . . What, you don't care about Ella Quinn anymore?"

At the mention of her name, Tyler's face scrunches up like he smells a fart.

"Ew, of course not. She's a waste of life, anyway."

I can't tell if he's telling the truth. Either Tyler actually doesn't care, and he's forgotten all about how angry he was, or it's more serious than that and he doesn't want it to show. Maybe his Ella Quinn feelings were also Big Feelings.

I look around the room. Miss A still isn't here, but when teachers are late, usually other teachers pop their heads in and out of the room to make sure no one is, like, murdered. Carefully, when Tyler's busy looking over his shoulder to make sure no one's watching us, I pull my phone out of my jeans pocket and swipe to the camera. I hit record and start talking.

"So are you going to stop what you were doing then?" I ask.

Tyler looks confused. "What do you mean?"

"The stuff on Ella Quinn's I Wonder. Are you going to stop messaging her?"

He laughs. "Why would I do that? It's fun. She gets all freaked out and it makes her look so stupid. Watching you guys run around like headless chickens all last week trying to bust me for it was *hilarious*. Thanks for that."

So it was the second option, then. Big Feelings. Tyler's going to pretend that he doesn't care about Ella Quinn while still terrorizing her every chance he gets.

"So you don't even have a reason to hurt her like this?" I ask. "You're just doing it to kill time?"

Tyler laughs. Not at me, really. He laughs like he thinks we're both laughing together. Because why wouldn't I be on his side? Everyone else is.

"Pretty much, yeah."

I snap.

I don't know how else to describe it. I snap, completely. I get right up in Tyler's face and I say things that I don't think I've *ever* said before. Y'know how in old cartoons they would pretend characters were swearing by having numbers and symbols and squiggly lines come out of their mouths?

It's like that, except there aren't any squiggly lines. Just me.

Look, I can't exactly repeat what I said to him. But for the sake of being thorough, let's just replace every bad word with the word *cheesecake*. Okay?

"Are you *cheesecake* kidding me? You actually *cheesecake* think that you're just going to keep *cheesecake* going around doing this *cheesecake* to Ella Quinn and you're going to get away with it? *Cheesecake* listen to me: I'm going to do whatever I *cheesecake* can to make sure you and your nasty *cheesecake* friends never get away with this *cheesecake* ever *cheesecake* again. If I have to dedicate my whole *cheesecake* life to it I *cheesecake* will, you disgusting, worthless, waste-of-space *cheesecake* CHEESECAKE!"

At first, Tyler looks impressed by me. Then he starts laughing, like I'm his pet dog who learned how to do a funny trick. Almost like it's cute and sweet that little quiet nothing Hazel can swear. That makes me even angrier. I can't see anything except Tyler. I stand up—

—and feel a tap on my shoulder.

"Normally, I'd ask you what you think you're doing," Mr. Pitts says. "But there's *never* an excuse for language like that."

Oh, cheesecake.

All the blood rushes out of my face. I've never been in real trouble before. When I pushed Tyler it didn't feel like actual trouble, since Tyler covered for me. This does. My eyes start to burn and all I can think is *don't cry, don't cry, do NOT cry in front of Tyler.*

"I was trying to . . . he's . . . Look!"

I pull out my phone, ready to show Mr. Pitts the recording. Even if I still get in trouble for the language, I don't care—it'll be worth it if this is what finally makes Mrs. West believe us.

But when I look at the screen, there's no video. I must have missed the record button because I was in such a rush.

"Great!" Mr. Pitts says, fake happy. "You can go straight down to the office and I'll go ahead and take that."

He yanks my phone out of my hand. Tyler looks at me, takes in my red face and shaking hands and the fact that I'm actually breathing hard after all of that, and laughs right in my face.

He goes back to doodling in his notebook like nothing even happened, and I go to the office. Again.

25

West called my parents.

Last time, it was easy to talk to my mom about the detention situation. She signed a form, I stayed inside one lunch, and everyone could just move on. Neither of my parents has said anything, and since I told them I was taking care of it, they didn't seem to question it. We'd worked out a system that was going really well for me.

This time, though, I have detention for a week. Mrs. West pretends that she's doing me a favor by not making it an in-school suspension, but I know she wouldn't even be able to because I'm the one kid in this school who actually read the parent handbook and I know foul language can only be punished with up to two weeks of lunchtime detention. I just barely resist rolling my eyes at her as she says it. I sit with my arms crossed in her stupid cushy office chairs and look everywhere but at her until she tells me that she called my mom.

She *called my mom* first thing in the morning when she was at work. My mom couldn't come into school right away, so I have to suffer through the whole day, dreading the meeting Mrs. West had scheduled after school. When it's finally time to face the music, my mom comes into West's office and looks at me like I've just robbed a bank. She thanks Mrs. West for her time, which is ridiculous because Mrs. West isn't doing her job and I'm pretty sure my mom was when Mrs. West called her this morning, so whose time are we *really* wasting here?

After the meeting, it takes my mom a long time to say anything to me. We both sit in the car and she drives us home and neither of us wants to be the first person to speak. Technically, I guess I'm supposed to apologize, but I don't really want to. I don't feel sorry. In fact, I feel like I've got a few more *cheesecakes* left in me if anyone tries to tell me again how good Tyler is. I shouldn't have said any of what I said (at least not within hearing range of a teacher, anyway), but I was starting to feel like a can of soda someone was shaking and shaking. Eventually I was going to explode.

"You have to sign that form again," I say quietly when we pull up to the house. My dad's car is in the driveway, which means he came home from work early just to yell at me. Awesome.

My mom doesn't answer, which is how I know she's *really* mad. I actually gulp when I walk inside and find my dad sitting on the couch in the living room.

"We're not mad at you," he says super quickly, which I'm pretty sure means he *is* mad at me. He and my mom have clearly held a strategy meeting and decided that saying they aren't mad will make them sound cooler and more approachable.

"But we'd like to have a conversation about what happened today," my mom says.

If they've rehearsed things this much, I must *really* be in trouble.

"Okay." I sit down in my dad's armchair and curl up into a ball.

"I know not too long ago we were talking, and you said you thought that we thought that you didn't have any friends, right?" my dad asks.

I nod.

"Honestly Hazel, we were a little worried about that," my mom says. "We would never think you're . . . Well, how did you put it?"

"I believe the phrase I used was 'friendless loser,'" I say.

My mom winces. "Exactly. We'd never think that! But we did notice that when you started middle school, it seemed like something changed. You weren't going to your friends' houses anymore. You just wanted to stay in your room."

"What does this have to do with today?" I ask. I don't need my parents talking about how few friends I have on top of everything else that's going on. If they're going to yell at me, I'd much rather they just get started already.

"We're just explaining why we were so excited when you asked to sleep over at Ella Quinn's house," my dad says. "We thought it would be great for you to have a friend—especially a friend like her. Someone who cares about the same things you do. She won the speech contest last year, right?"

I nod.

"And we also know that when you have a new friend, some-times you really want to make them happy," my mom says.

"What's that supposed to mean?" I ask.

"Your friend Tyler's mom called us," my dad says.

"What?!"

"She told us that she's worried that this Ella Quinn girl might be taking advantage of you," my mom explains. "She says she's seen this kind of thing before with Tyler. She told us it's very common for a popular girl like Ella Quinn to—"

"To what?" I demand. "To take some poor friendless freak like me under her wing?"

"That's not what we're saying," my dad says.

"Well, no, it is," I tell him. "It's what everyone's been saying to me lately, and I'd appreciate it if someone would just come right out and speak their mind. If it's so common for *popular girls like Ella Quinn* to be bad influences on less popular girls, that makes me the less popular girl, right? The loser who's so desperate for friends that she'll do whatever Ella asks? If you actually wanted to have a talk, why not ask me why I was so frustrated with Tyler? Why not *ask me* what's going on and actually *listen* to me when I tell you?"

My parents give each other a look. I hate that look.

"Tyler's mom also told us that Ella Quinn and Tyler went to the movies together once," my mom says.

"Oh my *god*," I say. "Ew. *EW!* You think I *like* Tyler?"

"That's perfectly normal!" my mom says. "I've been waiting

for you to tell me about your first crush since you started middle school!"

I take a deep breath. "Please listen to me," I say. "I feel like I'm going crazy. I shouldn't have used that kind of language at school, but everything that's going on became way too much. I just exploded."

Neither of my parents say anything for a second. Then, my mom's face lights up.

"Oh!" she says. She widens her eyes at my dad. He looks confused, and then my mom puts her hand up to her face and mouths something to him.

"Oh!" he says. "Hazel, I think I hear your brother. I'm going to go check on him."

He basically sprints out of the room, and then it's just me and my mom. She smiles at me. The whole tone shifts. I don't feel like I'm in trouble anymore, but I don't exactly feel at ease, either. Everything's gone weirdly quiet.

"You feel like you're going to explode?" she asks. She pats the spot on the couch beside her and I all but collapse down into it.

I breathe out a sigh of relief. Not a single adult has actually listened to me in weeks.

"Yes," I say, leaning into her side. "It's been so awful. It feels like no one even wants to listen to what I have to say."

My mom nods. "Are you feeling like that more often? A little more irritable?"

I frown. "I guess a little. But, I mean, the last few weeks have been extra irritating, so it's hard to tell."

She smiles at me. It's a weird smile, like she saw it in a movie and now she's trying to do it herself.

"Middle school can be *totally* weird," she says. "Have you noticed any other changes? To your mood or . . . your body?"

For a second I have no idea what she's talking about, and then it hits me. I sit up, move away from her.

"Mom, are you asking me if I've started my period?"

"There's absolutely nothing to be embarrassed about!"

I'm left sitting there with my mouth gaping open. I'm really, *really* not usually at a loss for words with my parents. But I don't even know what to say anymore.

I could probably try to talk to her. I could tell her everything that's been going on and maybe then, finally, someone would believe us. Wouldn't that be great?

But what if she doesn't? What if she disappoints me the way everyone else has? It's one thing for a teacher to not listen to me. It's one thing for Tyler's mom to not listen to me. But I don't know if I could take it if my parents didn't listen to me. And now my mom thinks that for me to be different, for me to stand up for my friends, my *whole body* has to change? I have to have some kind of *hormonal imbalance?!* It doesn't exactly inspire confidence.

I get up and don't listen when my mom asks me to come back. I slam my door shut and scream into my pillow. It only feels better for a second.

26

"And then she asked me if I was being *irritable* because I *started my period.*"

"Shut up." Riley's laughing so hard her face has turned bright red.

"I swear! My dad *left the room* and she was all, *Hazel, have you noticed any changes in your body?*"

Riley shrieks and covers her face with both hands. It took a lot of convincing for my mom to drop me off at Riley's after I calmed down, especially since it's a school night. I had to apologize for my outburst, and I may have implied that I did, in fact, get my period so that she'd go easy on me. I don't really know what that's supposed to look like, but I made a lot of sad faces and she started treating me like I was made of glass. I think she might have even teared up a bit. I'll have to figure that out later. She finally agreed when I promised her that Ella Quinn wouldn't be there. I even told her that Riley was *also* starting to think Ella Quinn might be a bad influence and that went over *really* well.

Once my mom thought Riley and I were the Good Kids trying to escape Ella Quinn's wrath it was a breeze to get her to drive me to Riley's.

I know it's not good to lie to your parents, but it's also not good to assume your daughter is just hormonal whenever she tries to defend her friends. So here we are.

"Did you try to explain what was actually happening?" Riley asks.

I shake my head. "I couldn't stand it. Like, I'm supposed to reassure them that my *body* is working normally before I can have a conversation with them now?"

Riley doesn't push it, which is good because I'm already starting to feel bad about blowing up at my parents. I've never been one of those kids who feel like they can't talk to their mom and dad about stuff.

"Ella'll be here in like ten minutes," Riley says, looking down at her phone.

I'd been kind of worried when we came up with this plan. It meant I would have to be at Riley's before Ella Quinn, and I've never really hung out with Riley alone before. My mom was obsessed with her house on the way up—we had to drive through the woods and eventually I had to call Riley for directions because her house is in the middle of nowhere. Once we saw it, though, we knew it was worth it. I've seen glimpses of the place through the trees on the bus, but seeing it up close is a totally different story. Riley said that her mom designed it herself—the front is all wood-paneled with these massive windows. It looks like something out of a fairy tale, or at least that's what my mom kept saying before she left.

Riley's mom was out picking up dinner, so we went up to her room to wait. I definitely had my guesses about what Ella Quinn's room was going to look like, but I hadn't ever thought about Riley's. As it turns out, it's the coolest room in history.

She has one of those giant windows at the front of the house, and her mom built her a window seat surrounded by bookshelves. The walls are forest green, and she has a *queen-size bed*. There are hanging baskets of green plants dotted around and a soft woven rug on the floor. It looks like a grownup lives here.

"You are way too cool to be hanging out with me," I said when I was done staring at everything.

Riley laughed and nudged me with her side.

"Back atcha," she said, and then we both laughed, and it was like I'd been going to her house for years.

Riley turned on her record player (because of course she has a record player) and now we're both sprawled out on her bed while the music plays. I couldn't wait for Ella Quinn to get here before I told Riley what happened with my parents — some things are too ridiculous to wait.

"I think my mom would rather cover herself in bacon grease and leave herself out for the coyotes than talk to me about my period," Riley says.

"She was so *excited about it*." I shudder. "Like, has she just been *waiting* this whole time?"

Riley covers her face with her hands and both of us collapse onto her bed laughing.

I hear a car pull up Riley's driveway, but both of us are so comfortable that neither of us moves. The door clicks open and a woman's voice yells, "I found a stray!"

Riley yells back, "Is it shaped like Ella, or is this like that time you found a baby raccoon?"

I've never heard Riley yell before. She's a totally different person in this house, in her own world. I like it. And I'd like more information about that baby raccoon.

"It's shaped like Ella," Ella Quinn says from the door. She has her pink backpack on and she's carrying a massive book from the adult section of the library that I don't go to very often because the books are dusty and set off my asthma.

"Hey!" Riley says, lifting her head off the bed and waving her over. "Guess what? Hazel's *a woman* now."

"Shut up!" I laugh. Ella Quinn raises her eyebrows at us, but doesn't ask questions.

"More on that later," she says. "We have work to do, ladies!" She even claps her hands like she's a teacher.

Riley and I look at each other. She looks as worn-out as I feel.

"I don't know if I have the energy to burn Tyler to the ground tonight," I say. "I tried that earlier and all it got me was a week of detention."

"Not *him*," Ella Quinn says. "I can't even *think* about him right now. Hazel, do you realize the speech competition is on *Friday*? As in *this* Friday?"

I knew that. The closer we get to winter break, the louder and messier all of the classrooms become. It's a very annoying week to have detention, really—if we were actually doing work in class, I'd have something to do with my time. We had a *Frozen* sing-along in geography the other day. So I know, objectively, that the speech competition is this Friday. Hearing Ella Quinn say it, though, makes it more real. A bit of the old me, the version who only cared about winning the speech contest at all costs, comes back. I thought it would be weird being friends with Ella Quinn while still also wanting to beat her at the speech competition, but she hasn't made it weird at all. And if she hasn't made it weird, then that means I can play to win and still keep her around as a friend.

"If I'm going to kick your butt, I have to start memorizing! We have to rehearse! We have to both bribe Riley with more and more candy and personal favors until she chooses a winner!"

"I'm not doing that," Riley points out. Ella ignores her.

"I haven't practiced my speech in . . ." I trail off when I realize I don't actually *know* when the last time I practiced my speech was. I feel the blood drain from my face. "Oh god."

"Exactly!" Ella Quinn says. "I have a winning legacy to continue. I'd much rather you give me a fight than just give up like this. It would be a hollow victory."

"Who says it's going to be a victory?" I start to smile and Riley rolls her eyes at us. "You may have a winning legacy to continue, but I have a *vendetta*."

"Riley, may I just say that you look absolutely *beautiful* today?" Ella Quinn says, batting her eyelashes at her.

"Enough!" Riley laughs. "I'll sit and provide pointers and ask questions, but I will *not* be picking a winner."

"Deal." Ella Quinn grins, but then goes serious again. "I just . . . I really want to have something that makes me happy, y'know? The speech competition was so much fun to do last year. I want to try to feel the way I did then. I just want to focus on that. Maybe I can *actually* have fun again. Maybe I can feel normal again."

Riley and I look at each other. I didn't realize that's what the competition meant to Ella Quinn. I just liked doing it because it was one of the only things at our school that I could win — it's not like I was about to join the volleyball team with Bella or set a new long jump record.

"All right then," I say. I get up, grabbing Riley by the arm with me. We both sit in Riley's window seat. I sit straight up and give Ella my best Serious Grownup Face. "Wow me."

Ella Quinn smiles like that's the best thing she's ever heard.

27

For the first time ever, I spend a morning waiting for the bell to ring.

Don't get me wrong, it's not like I slack off. I don't think I'll ever be the kind of girl to just sit there and doodle on her binder or try to secretly text her friends during class. But even while I'm taking notes and writing down homework assignments and running through my speech for the billionth time in my head, I'm thinking about getting through the morning. All I have to do is sit in today's lunch detention before I have class with Ella Quinn and Riley.

When the bell finally rings, I'm way too excited about going to detention. I don't even care if it's Mr. Pitts supervising. I only need to get to the end of lunch. You can do anything for one lunch period. It's just that I have to do this particular thing for five lunch periods.

On my way out to detention and, eventually, freedom, though, Miss A stops me.

"Hazel, would you mind sticking around for a second?" she asks. "I have something I wanted to chat with you about."

Kaden overhears and goes *ooooooh* in a fake-girly high-pitched voice. God, at least try to be *creative*. Miss A cuts her eyes at him and he scurries off. Ugh, I can't wait to be an adult and to be able to shut down Kadens and Tylers. I enjoy a very brief fantasy during which I'm a teacher and a girl like Ella Quinn comes to me with a problem and I get the boy expelled from every school ever, forever, because I'm an adult and some adults have a lot of power, and I think I'd *very much* enjoy being the kind of adult with a lot of power.

"I actually have to go . . ." I start to say to Miss A, but I trail off. I'm sure she knows exactly where I have to go. The thing about adults is that they'll usually trust each other before they'll trust a kid. Even the nice adults (Miss A) would sooner talk to the meanest adults (Mr. Pitts) before they'd talk to a kid (me). I'm sure Mr. Pitts has already told her all about how terrible I am, and I don't really want to remind Miss A that I'm in detention-worthy trouble for the second time this month.

"I'll put in a good word with the detention supervisor." She tries to wink again and still doesn't quite land it. "I just wanted to ask you how your speech was coming along. You're still participating, right?"

"Of course I am!" I say, horrified at the idea of missing the speech competition. It's only the *only thing* I thought of all summer. "I think it's going really well so far. I like my topic a lot."

"Remind me of it?"

I stand up straighter and try to use a Professional Voice. "Unsolved mysteries of the twentieth century. I think it's gonna be really interesting."

Miss A smiles at me. I know teachers aren't supposed to have favorites, but I think I might be hers. At least one adult in this school seems to like me.

Ella Quinn and I practiced our speeches for *hours* yesterday. Honestly, I'm not sure how Riley got through it. She refused to pick a winner, like she promised, but then after I got home, way after I was supposed to be asleep, my phone buzzed. Riley texted *I think you won* and I had to hide my face under my pillow for a solid five minutes.

Because I'm glad my speech was good. Not because of any other reason that may need to be examined at a later date. There's simply no time for that right now.

"Sounds great," Miss A says. "I'm really looking forward to hearing it. I think the speech contest is a really wonderful way for you guys to find your voice, y'know?"

"Yeah," I say. I mean, I guess. You literally have to use your voice to participate, so I see where she's going with that. I can tell Miss A is preparing for another rant about something, though, so I just have to buckle up.

"A great speech can change the world. If you have something to say, and you say it well, you might find it's the perfect way to get a point across. Even if it scares you."

"Sure," I say. Sometimes Miss A gets this far-off look in her eyes like she's really trying hard to impart wisdom into today's youth. I guess she might be imparting wisdom right now, but I think I'd have to understand what she's talking about to really get the full effect.

"You must be getting excited!" she says then. "Only a few more days to go. Did you know the local paper covers this round of the competition? And I think I heard that a school board representative will be there, too. A very fancy woman. Mrs. West's boss's boss."

I think I finally get what she's saying. My face flushes and I duck my head. Suddenly I can't look Miss A in the eye.

"Don't worry," I tell her. "I won't mess up like I did last year. I made my parents check my pronunciation of every word."

"Oh!" Miss A says. "No, I didn't mean anything like that."

"What did you mean, then?"

Miss A smiles at me, but not in that proud way she does when I understand her rants.

"Well!" she says instead of answering my question. She claps her hands the way Ella Quinn did last night. "Shall we escort each other to detention?"

We both walk out of the classroom together and head down the hall to Mr. Pitts's room, where detention is always held. I think he likes having a Sad Energy in there.

Now that I know Miss A is the detention supervisor, I feel even better about getting through lunch. I'll have an hour to work on my speech, and then I'm home free.

But when Miss A and I walk into the detention room, I stop dead in my tracks.

Ella Quinn is sitting at one of the desks. She looks up when she hears us come in, and she tries to smile at me, but it's all wrong. She's obviously been crying—her face is red and her blue eyes are still watery.

"Oh!" Miss A says suddenly. "I forgot my knitting in my classroom. Talk among yourselves!"

I love Miss A sometimes.

As soon as she leaves, I whip my head toward Ella Quinn.

"What happened?" I demand. "What's wrong?"

Ella Quinn's lip wobbles and she puts her head in her arms on her desk.

"I'm the ringleader," she says. It comes out muffled, so I have to really strain to hear her, but I don't ask her to lift her head up because it doesn't really seem like she can. "That's what Tyler told his mom. I'm going after him, and I'm putting you up to things. So I got detention too."

She keeps her head in her arms, and I hear her sniffle. I know Ella Quinn isn't used to getting detention, but I've never seen her this upset.

"Detention isn't so bad!" I say. "Especially not when it's Miss A supervising. She'll let us do work. I bet if we asked, we could practice our speeches!"

That's when Ella *really* starts crying. Shoulders-shaking, puddle-forming, nose-dripping kind of crying.

"But I'm *the ringleader*, right?" She finally looks up at me and her face is a mess. "I'm the ringleader, and I need to be made an example of. So I get your punishment, plus something extra. I can't compete in the speech contest."

My stomach drops. For a second, I think I must have misheard her. There's no way the school would make Ella Quinn drop out of the speech contest. Miss A said it herself: everyone goes to the speech competition. Why wouldn't they want someone like Ella to be part of it?

Then it hits me. Miss A already knew about all of this. She knew Ella Quinn wouldn't be allowed to compete. That's why she was talking about everyone that was going to be at the competition, and how important speeches are.

Now I get what she was trying to say.

28

It's one thing to be told that a lot of people are going to be at the speech competition. It's *really* another thing to be sitting in an uncomfortable plastic chair on the gym stage while roughly three million people file in and sit on the bleachers.

First thing in the morning, there's an announcement for the competitors to report to the gym. Everyone is told the rules (as if we don't already know them) and then we draw numbers to see who gets to go first. Generally, you want to go first or last, so the closer you can get to first or last the better. Initially when I draw the spot for second to last, I'm excited. That would have been my ideal spot at the beginning of the week. I would have been confident. I would have joked with Ella Quinn, bragging about getting such a good slot. But everything's different now. Ella Quinn will be walking into the gym with the rest of Mr. Pitts's class, not on the stage where she belongs.

Everyone in the whole school gets out of class and comes to watch the competition. They get yelled at by their teachers if they don't pay attention. *Good.* That's what I've needed this whole time: the right person's attention.

I scan the crowd and spot Mrs. West right away, sitting beside a tall lady I don't recognize. Mrs. West keeps laughing too loudly at everything she says, so either this is the world's weirdest first date or she's the school board rep. Mrs. West's boss's boss.

Ella Quinn and Riley are here somewhere, but I can't find them. They're sitting with Mr. Pitts's class in the bleachers and I know that just seeing the stage set up, thinking there should be a chair for her up here, is killing Ella. It's killing me, too. Last year I was happy to not have any distractions while I was competing. I remember rolling my eyes when the other kids were talking to their friends or trying to get their attention, waving at them from the stage. I remember thinking *that's not going to win you any competitions.*

But now I'd really like it if my friend were beside me.

Mrs. West walks up onto the stage, her knee-high boots clicking like thunder. She welcomes everyone to the competition and talks about how wonderful it is to work at a school where the students are so involved and intelligent. I don't think I hide the look of disgust on my face very well, but she's standing in front of me so it's not like she can see it.

From there, nothing weird happens, I'm pretty sure. Everyone gets through their speeches, I think. No one falls or does their speech on sex or anything else memorable. We won't be laughing at someone for the rest of the year for accidentally saying *pubic* instead of *public*.

But I couldn't tell you what anyone's speeches are about. I could only tell you about my pounding heart, my shaking knees, and my difficulty breathing as my turn gets closer and closer. I think for sure I won't be able to do what I'm planning on doing.

The first time I question my plan comes in the middle of the second speech, given by a guy in the sixth grade who I don't know. I look at his back, at his confident posture, and wonder who he is. Do all his teachers think he's extra special? Does his mom think he could never do anything wrong?

The second time happens during the sixth speech, halfway through the competition. It's a girl in eighth grade with long copper hair falling in big curls down to her waist. Did boys pull on her hair at recess? Did her teachers tell her that they probably just liked her?

The third time happens during speech number ten. The last one before I go. I look out into the audience. I can't see him, but I know that Tyler's out there. Probably whispering unfunny jokes to his friends, who'll laugh at them anyway. I can see Mrs. West, though. I've known exactly where she is this entire time. I glance over at her, and seeing her expressionless face as she listens to the speech sends a wave of anxiety through me. I saw what Mrs. West did to Ella Quinn when we told her about Tyler. But that time, nobody else could hear us. What would she do if I talked about Tyler where *everyone* could hear me?

Scattered applause breaks me out of my panic. That's the one downside of performing near the end of the competition: people get tired of clapping for you. But I guess I don't need much cheering and clapping for what I'm about to do.

I know that it's my turn, but I can barely get out of my chair. I wasn't nervous like this last year. I knew what I was going to say and it was easy. Now, my knees are knocking together and when I get up to the microphone, I'm not sure if I'll even be able to speak. But I know I have to. I know this one last plan might be the thing that actually works. I know I need to try. I clear my throat and step up to the mic.

"Have you ever experienced something you just couldn't explain?" I start my speech the way I was always going to. "Maybe you think you saw flashing lights in the sky one night, or even a ghost. There are some mysteries out there that have been around for years, and many of them are still unsolved today."

I could keep going. I could finish my speech, and I might even win the contest. I know it's good. I know it's *great*.

But I look out into the audience one more time, and I finally spot Ella Quinn and Riley. They both give me a big thumbs-up. I know it's breaking Ella Quinn's heart to see me up here, but she still wants me to do well.

I look down at my notecards. I have the old speech memorized, but this one was only written last night.

"But . . ." I clear my throat, take a deep breath. "But the biggest mystery in my life right now is why boys like Tyler Harris are being allowed to sexually harass and belittle girls that go to this school. Maybe even the girl you're sitting beside right now. Maybe even you."

I pick a spot at the very back of the gym where I can't see anyone. No one jumps up onto the stage and drags me off. I keep going.

"A study done at the University of Illinois found that one in four students experiences some kind of verbal or physical sexual harassment during their time in middle school. The American Association of University Women found an even more troubling statistic—nearly half of students in grades seven to twelve have been harassed. This harassment is believed to be underreported. Maybe because no one thinks kids in middle school are old enough to think and act like this. Most people still see us as little kids.

"I have a friend. I know that sounds pretty basic, like, of course I have a friend. But, honestly, having friends is kind of new to me. A month ago, that friend started getting anonymous questions on her I Wonder account. But not the way you're *supposed* to get anonymous questions on your I Wonder account. They were horrible. Sexual, threatening, and intimidating. They scared me, so I can't even imagine how they must have scared her. That same study from the AAUW found that 37 percent of the girls who were harassed felt physically sick after. And 34 percent had trouble studying. Harassment like this leads to more absences, poor grades, and other behavioral problems that never would have happened otherwise."

I'm too nervous to see Mrs. West's reaction, and I don't

actually know if Ella Quinn is going to appreciate this or not. I'm not being subtle. Everyone knows that I only hang out with Ella Quinn and Riley. Riley doesn't date. It wouldn't take a genius to figure out exactly who I'm talking about.

Since I can't look at the audience, I take a breath and look up at the ceiling for a second before I start again.

"I *know* that Tyler is the one who sent my friend those messages. I can prove it, and he told me himself, multiple times. He's proud of it. He bragged about it, to my face. Twice. We went to Mrs. West for help, because that's what we're supposed to do, right? You find a grownup and they take care of things. Instead, we were the ones who were punished. We were told that we needed to be safer online. My friend was told to *act more like a little girl.* That if she did that, maybe she wouldn't need to worry about having problems like this. But if we're little girls, don't we deserve protection? If we're *people,* don't we deserve to feel safe?"

I lock eyes with Bella Blake in the audience for a second. She's grinning ear to ear and mouths *go on* at me. I try to hide my smile.

"I love this contest. I know that's nerdy, but I had so much fun last year, and I was so excited to compete again this year. My parents don't really get why I love it so much. I don't think I got it either, until last week. I love this contest because it's one of the only times people *have* to listen to me. I think that's why my friend likes it, too. She should be up here beside me, but even though she did everything right and went to a teacher when Tyler was harassing her, she was the one who was punished. And now this one opportunity, these three to five minutes when people actually have to listen to what you have to say for once, was taken away from her.

"I thought I might even be able to win the contest this year. I'm not telling you that to brag. I'm trying to show you what it takes to do this. To tell you what's happening. I wouldn't be saying any of this if it wasn't one hundred percent true. All we want is to be believed."

I take another breath.

"We see the way the adults in our life react when someone comes forward about sexual harassment. We notice that you might make some comment about an actress looking to boost her career when she speaks out about a director. We hear people asking what a girl was wearing when she was assaulted. When we come to you and you don't believe us, we know what that means. We learn what we mean to you."

I finally look down at Mrs. West. Her face is practically purple. I can't believe she hasn't come up here and dragged me off the stage herself. But the woman beside her, the school board rep, her boss's boss, is looking at me with tears in her eyes.

I look her in the eye when I say, "Please believe us."

Before I can even turn around and sit down, Miss A stands up in her seat and starts clapping so loudly, it sounds like ten people. Ella Quinn and Riley join in quickly, whooping and cheering. Bella the Beast stands up and whistles. For a second, I think it's going to be one of those movie moments where the whole school gives me a standing ovation, but then I remember that this is the real world. What actually happens is a couple of eighth grade girls also stand up, but everyone else claps politely and I sit back down.

The last competitor, a boy named Carlos in my homeroom who's now looking at me like I might eat him alive, starts to get up. But before he makes it to the mic, Mrs. West hurries onto the stage and grabs it from him.

"Boys and girls," she says, and then cuts herself off, looking at where the school board rep is watching her with narrowed eyes. "I mean, students. Obviously, after that . . . unprecedented speech from Miss Hill, we need to take a brief break. Would Tyler Harris please go to my office immediately, and, Hazel, if you wouldn't mind joining us as well? I'm sorry to miss the final speech of the competition, but I'm sure everyone here can understand the magnitude of the situation."

Yeah, I think, *everyone but you, apparently.* I've never seen Mrs. West look so flustered before. I kind of love that it happened because of me.

I follow Mrs. West off the stage, pretending like the whole school *isn't* watching me and whispering to each other, wondering if I'm going to get in trouble or if I'm going to forever be known as the girl who got Tyler Harris expelled.

Mrs. West makes it to the gym door, where Tyler's waiting. He doesn't seem to have anything to say to me right now. He looks small. Meek. The way he's been making Ella Quinn feel. Neither of us says anything to the other as we walk out of the gym and down the hall to the office with Mrs. West. The school board rep walks with us, just a little bit behind Mrs. West. When we get to the office, she touches my shoulder, just for a second.

"That was a very, *very* brave thing you did."

I feel like I could collapse right then and there. If she's calling me brave, does that mean she believes us? Does that mean something's going to actually happen?

"Wait here for just a second," the school board rep tells me. "Will you be okay?"

I don't know what she's talking about until I realize she's asking if I'll be okay sitting beside Tyler. If I'm comfortable with it. She cares enough about the situation to think that I might be uncomfortable sitting beside Tyler! I feel like I'm floating, the way walking feels in dreams.

"I'll be fine." I smile at her and she smiles back, and then she and Mrs. West disappear into West's office.

"Kiss-ass," Tyler mutters. He's slumped in a chair and I roll my eyes and sit in the one beside him. I wasn't lying to the school board rep—I'm not afraid to sit beside Tyler. I've never been afraid of Tyler. The problem was that Tyler didn't understand that he should have been afraid of *me*.

"You can be as mad at me as you want," I say. "If you didn't want me to call you out in front of the whole school, you should have stopped when we told you to."

"Whatever." Tyler rolls his eyes.

I can't lie, I'm feeling pretty good about the situation. The school board rep seems to be on my side and, at the very least,

Tyler must be feeling a bit embarrassed. That's what makes me so confident when I reply to him.

"Y'know, I read the school handbook the summer before sixth grade. Have you ever read it?"

Tyler gives me a look. I still know him well enough to know that look means *obviously not, and you're stupid for even asking.*

"Yeah, didn't think so. Anyway, there's a whole section about punishments in it. Like, what you have to do to get expelled, what happens if you spray-paint a teacher's car, that kind of thing. There's a sexual harassment section—"

"What *does* happen if you spray-paint a teacher's car?"

"Probably nothing close to what they'll do to you for this."

Tyler goes quiet at that and I think maybe, finally, I've won. But then, of course, he opens his mouth again.

"I thought we were friends," he says.

I give him my best unamused face. "No, you didn't. You thought I was someone you could use as a human diary. And now that we aren't surrounded by your friends and your mom can't bail you out, you're starting to worry you might actually face a consequence. And you don't even know what the consequence might be. I just tried to tell you and you changed the subject and spoke over me. The way you always do."

He could be expelled for this. That's what I was trying to tell him. The handbook says that if sexual harassment can be "objectively proven," then the student can be expelled.

Maybe I'll let that be a little surprise for just Tyler.

"Tyler." Mrs. West leans out of her office door. "Come in, please."

Tyler stands up and looks at me for a second, like he's going to say something. I guess he changes his mind, because he just rolls his eyes at me and walks off, leaving me alone in the office. Well, unless you count Mr. Vickers and his wiener dog shrine.

I put my chin in my hands. I hadn't realized vengeance would require so much waiting around.

"Hazel?"

I look up at the sound of my name, expecting to see Mrs. West or another teacher, but instead, Brooklyn is standing in the office doorway.

"Hi," I say.

Brooklyn takes that as an invitation, stepping fully into the office and sitting in the chair beside me.

"So, Tyler told me about how he's gonna go for it with Rebecca," she says. I grimace.

"Yeah, he told me that too."

Brooklyn nods and then tilts her head back to look up at the ceiling.

"I feel kind of stupid," she says.

"You're not stupid," I say. "He's stupid. Didn't you hear my speech? That was, like, the whole point of it."

Brooklyn laughs. "'Now presenting my speech: Tyler Harris is stupid.'"

"'Tyler Harris is stupid. End of speech. Thank you for your time.'"

We both laugh again.

"That one probably would've won," Brooklyn says.

I tilt my head. Honestly, I'd forgotten that there was an actual competition going on as soon as I started talking. My speech was definitely less than three minutes long, so I wouldn't have even been eligible to win.

Brooklyn rubs the back of her neck awkwardly. She looks at me sideways, like she can't quite face me full-on.

"Sorry. About . . . y'know. All of it."

I shrug. "You should probably apologize to Ella Quinn, not me."

"Yeah, I will."

We both sit there in silence for a couple of seconds, and then Brooklyn gets up.

"Pitts thinks I'm in the bathroom," she explains, and then runs off.

That's fair. I think if it weren't specifically illegal, Pitts would whip his class.

The bell rings. The halls are about to be filled up with kids rushing off to their next class. Somewhere, Ella Quinn and Riley are going to science without me, probably wondering what's going on and whether we're being taken seriously.

It feels like Tyler's been in West's office forever. I try counting how many bedazzled picture frames Mr. Vickers has on his desk but lose count after twenty. The longer Tyler's in there, the more nervous I get. The school board rep seemed really smart and nice, but Tyler managed to fool plenty of other teachers before. Maybe he's charming her the way he charms everyone else. Maybe by the time he gets out of West's office, I'll be the one in trouble again.

A loud knock on the office window snaps me out of it. Mr. Vickers startles, looking up and glaring at me like it was my fault. I whip around at the noise and before I can help it, a smile creeps onto my face.

There's Ella Quinn, grinning wider than I've ever seen.

"Holy crap," she says, and I burst out laughing.

29

Mrs. West's office looks a little nicer when she's being yelled at in it.

"The fact that this young woman felt like she had to stand up in front of the *entire school* just to get your attention? For something this serious? Did you ask the boy *any* questions, or just assume from the get-go these twelve-year-olds were lying to you?"

The more the school board rep (her name is Ms. Gates and she's my new hero) asks, the further Mrs. West slumps down into her seat. Tyler's being suspiciously quiet, sitting with his arms crossed in the corner like a toddler having a temper tantrum. Ms. Gates was the one to call me into the office, just before I could ask Ella Quinn if she was *really* sure that what I did was okay. Ms. Gates didn't look as stern as she did when we all walked to the office. She smiled at me again and my heart lifted up, just a little bit, at the thought that Tyler had finally met a grownup who didn't immediately fall for his innocent act.

I think I want to be Ms. Gates when I grow up.

"I'm sure you can understand the difficult position it put me in," Mrs. West tries to say. "What with Tyler's mother's . . . role."

Plot twist: Tyler's mom is the school district's superintendent. She's basically Mrs. West's boss. But Ms. Gates is her boss's boss, remember? So Ms. Gates isn't afraid of anyone. *Especially* not Tyler Harris's mom.

"I don't care if Tyler's mother is the Queen of England. If a student comes to you feeling unsafe, you make them feel safe. If you don't understand that, I truly can't comprehend why you would become an educator in the first place. Surely you realize that I would have backed you one hundred percent. Why else would I be in this job?"

"Well, you must know that Mrs. Harris can be—"

"Mrs. Harris can be *what*, exactly?"

I whip my head around and my jaw drops. Tyler's mom is standing in the doorway. Her perfect hair from the other day is gone. It looks like she's been screaming. She must have flown here on her broom really quickly to already be in the office.

(Sorry, I take that back. That's offensive to witches.)

"Mrs. Harris." Ms. Gates nods at her. "Sorry to call you in on such short notice, but I'm sure you realize the seriousness of this situation."

"I understand the seriousness of this . . . *campaign* against my son, yes," Mrs. Harris says. "I'm glad to see you have this *girl* here." She points at me. "Where are the other two?"

She says *girl* the way other people might say *slug* or *boiled eyeball* or *dog poo*.

"Hazel's, Ella Quinn's, *and* Riley Beckett's parents have been called, and they're on their way," Ms. Gates says.

My heart sinks. "They didn't do anything wrong!" I say. It's the first time I've spoken since Ms. Gates asked me to come into the office ten minutes ago.

"Their parents have been called so that I can offer my apologies in person," Ms. Gates continues. She smiles at me and my shoulders finally relax. I think I might cry.

"Your *apologies?*" Mrs. Harris demands. "Where's the apology for *my son?*"

Oh, I could tell her where to stick an apology for her son. But that doesn't feel like a good idea in front of Ms. Gates.

Suddenly, the phone on Mrs. West's desk starts ringing. She picks it up, and I watch as the color drains from her face. She hands the phone to Ms. Gates wordlessly.

"Yes?" Ms. Gates asks the person on the other end of the phone. As she listens, her lips purse. Her forehead starts to wrinkle.

"I see," she says. "Thank you."

She hangs up and takes a deep, deep breath. After, she looks up at Tyler's mom.

"Mrs. Harris, did you notice anything unusual in the office when you stormed in here?" Ms. Gates says.

Tyler's mom doesn't answer her question, so Ms. Gates nods and stands up.

"Hazel, if you wouldn't mind? I'd like to show Mrs. Harris something, and I think you'd like to see it as well."

She escorts us out of Mrs. West's office and into the main office lobby, leaving Tyler behind to pout.

I see what that phone call was about the second we leave—it would be pretty hard to miss. I've never, *ever* seen the office like this. Not even last year when there was a rumor that a kid in seventh grade had formed a cult and all the parents showed up.

The place is *packed* full of girls.

Girls I know. Girls I don't know. Girls I recognize but can't place. Girls in my class and Mr. Pitts's class and sixth grade girls and eighth grade girls, including Tyler's most recent crush, Rebecca. Bella's here. Brooklyn's here. Maya isn't, but that's okay, because we'll do this for her.

"Ladies!" Ms. Gates calls, and the office goes silent. "Thank you so much for your time. We'll be speaking to every last one of you today and I can personally promise that we'll take each and every one of you seriously. In the meantime, though, if you're comfortable sharing, can I ask anyone here to voice a complaint about Tyler Harris to please raise their hand?"

Every single hand shoots up in the air.

"Well, you obviously can't believe *all of them* have been . . . what, rejected? By my son." Tyler's mom rolls her eyes. "You're going to let them all gang up on him like this? He's a *little boy*, you know how they can get at this age! It's practically *impossible* to raise a boy in this day and age! No one lets them just *be boys*. I've raised two others and, let me tell you, it wasn't always easy, but when there are . . . hiccups like this you just need to tell them that they're doing wonderfully and that everything will be okay."

"Tyler has not been doing wonderfully," Ms. Gates says. "And everything will *not* be okay as long as that's allowed to continue. Expulsion is not off the table. Suspension, certainly, is on it."

I smirk. Such a shame Tyler didn't listen to me when I tried to tell him exactly that!

Mrs. Harris doesn't seem to know how to respond. I don't think she has much experience with being told no either.

"We'll continue this conversation later," she says, but Ms. Gates shrugs casually, like it doesn't even matter what Tyler's mom thinks, and my smirk turns into a grin.

Mrs. Harris storms back into West's office and after a few minutes, emerges with Tyler in tow. The two of them barge their way through the sea of girls and out the front door. I've never been happy to see Tyler Harris's butt until it was leaving school in shame and defeat.

"Hazel!"

I freeze. Oh god.

My parents squeeze their way through the crowd of girls in the office and run right up to me. They both try to hug me at the same time, which is a little difficult when my mom is wearing Rowan on her front so both of us end up squished cheek to cheek.

This all happens in front of a *solid* portion of kids I go to school with. So that's fun.

"We are *so proud of you!*" my mom says. She's definitely been crying.

"We never should have doubted you," my dad says. I look at him like *yeah, I know,* and he laughs.

"We're sorry we didn't listen to you," my mom says. "We messed up."

"I'm so sorry to interrupt," Ms. Gates says, "but we do need to have a conversation about what happens next."

"Surely what happens next is that little creep gets expelled and our daughter can continue her education uninterrupted," my mom says. She tries to look menacing, but it's hard to do with Rowan drooling down his carrier.

Ms. Gates ushers us into West's office again and all of us squeeze in tightly. Maybe Mrs. West is so grumpy because her office is elf-size.

"I've already apologized to Hazel, but I'd also like to apologize to you two," Ms. Gates says to begin with. "I'm sure that when you sent your daughter to school here, you assumed that she'd be safe and cared for. I'm sorry that didn't happen to the absolute best of our ability in this case."

Ms. Gates grimaces. "You have my word that we'll be more closely monitoring these situations across the entire school district. You should be very proud of your daughter for the change she and her friends have brought."

That seems to pacify my parents a bit. Ms. Gates is good.

"What happens to Tyler now?" I ask. I know I shouldn't, but

I lean forward in my seat a little the way you do during a really good part in a movie.

Ms. Gates takes a big breath.

"I wish I could tell you everything will be different right away," she says. "But I can't guarantee anything."

That heavy feeling fills up my chest again.

"So Tyler can just get away with it all again?" I ask. "I read the school handbook! It says that proven cases of sexual harassment can be punished with expulsion."

Ms. Gates smiles like she can't help it, but this time it bugs me. When my parents look at me like that they usually think I'm being cute. I don't want to be cute. I want vengeance.

"It does say that," she agrees. "But there are a lot of people out there who would question whether this is a *proven* case of sexual harassment."

"How much more proof do you need?" I demand. "I've only spent the last *month* gathering evidence and being punished for it."

I've never spoken to a teacher like this before, let alone a member of the school board that governs the entire school district. There's just something in the air on speech day.

"Hazel," Ms. Gates says. "I want you to listen to me. I believe you. I believe you and your friends and every single girl out there. I promise to listen to all of them. But if you want Tyler to be punished for what he did, this is only the first step in a long process."

I slowly let out a long breath. I'm tired. Ella and Riley are tired.

I think about all of the girls standing out there in the office. I bet they're tired too. But maybe, if we all do this together, it won't be as tiring.

"What's step two?" I ask. My mom sniffles beside me. She's definitely fantasizing about my future presidency.

Ms. Gates smiles at me again, but not like she thinks I'm cute this time. Like she's impressed with me.

I like that one a lot more.

"How about this," she says. "Send in Ella so I can apologize to her, and you go and enjoy the rest of your day. I'll see you and your friends first thing Monday morning. We can go over everything then, but I think you've *more* than earned a little break from this."

I don't want to leave. I'm afraid that if I leave, whatever magic Ms. Gates is working right now is going to break, and everything will go back to the way it was before.

But then Ms. Gates takes her phone out of her pocket and opens her calendar. I guess school board members are busy people, because every day she has about a billion meetings and appointments. She holds her phone out to face me and I watch as she clears her schedule for Monday. She deletes every single event she had scheduled on her phone, and replaces all of them with just one: 8:00 a.m. — Oakridge — Hazel Hill.

"Okay?" she asks.

She's not solving everything the way I hoped that she would. But she's trying way more than anyone else has so far.

"Okay."

"I'll walk you out," Mrs. West says. She's been suspiciously quiet this whole time, but now she leaps into action. Unfortunately for her, Ms. Gates is faster.

"That won't be necessary, Mrs. West," she says. "You should be here to apologize to Miss Quinn yourself."

I just barely resist saying *ooooh*. It's not every day that your principal gets sent to the office.

"Let's get out of here," my dad says. He kisses me on the top of the head and I follow him into the school's lobby. It's just as chaotic out here as it was in the office. Everyone's teachers must have given up on keeping kids in class today.

"It's, like, barely noon," I say. "I still have my whole other half of classes today."

"Not today you don't," my dad says. "It's like Ms. Gates said: you deserve a break."

Through the crowd, I realize Ella Quinn and Riley are sitting in the big cushy armchairs in the lobby that someone must have thought makes the school look more welcoming. Both of their moms are standing behind them. Ella Quinn's mom has her hands on Ella's shoulders and it looks like she's ready to fight anyone who comes near either of them.

"I thought we could all go out for lunch," my mom says, half to me and half to Ella Quinn's and Riley's moms. "It would give us a chance to all get to know each other better. I get the sense we'll be seeing a lot more of one another."

"Ms. Gates wanted to see you in West's office," I tell Ella Quinn. "She wants to apologize for how messed up all of this has been."

"You mean I get to go into West's office and *not* get detention?" Ella Quinn asks. "I'm in."

"You guys can go on and we'll meet you there?" Ella Quinn's mom says.

"We can wait," I say immediately. I haven't left Ella Quinn and Riley behind during all of this and I'm not going to start now.

I take Ella Quinn's spot in the big chair while she and her mom make their way to the office. Rowan starts getting fussy, so my parents take him for a walk around the school.

But then something weird starts to happen. I look up, and realize people are watching me. The girls waiting outside the office to complain about Tyler all look at me like I'm someone impressive.

"I feel like a zoo animal," I mutter to Riley.

She laughs. "I think you're gonna have to get used to it. Everyone knows how cool you are now. But I realized it first, so you can't leave me for all of them when you start getting better offers."

I blush, but try to pretend like I'm not by laughing and covering my mouth with my hand.

"I'm not gonna leave you for a better offer," I say, and then cough. "You or Ella Quinn, I mean. Neither of you. You're both stuck with me now."

Riley lets her head fall back onto the chair and looks at me with a little smile.

"Good."

30

About an hour and a half later, once Ms. Gates has finished apologizing to Ella Quinn and her mom, we all go out to the lot, where our parents have parked beside each other.

"We're riding together," Ella Quinn says before anyone can get in a car. She puts one arm around Riley and one around me and sort of hangs off our shoulders since we're both taller than her. "Grownups can figure that out, just tell us which car to get in."

My mom has Rowan's car seat in her car, so my dad clicks the button on his keys to honk his horn and says, "All aboard!" which is embarrassing, but I'm feeling good, so I let it slide.

"I don't want to make this weird," my dad says when we're all in the car and my mom is talking to Ella Quinn's and Riley's moms about Mom Stuff in the parking lot, "but Hazel's mom and I also wanted to apologize to you, Just Ella."

"Oh my god, Dad, enough with the Just Ella." I put my head in my hands and absolutely do not turn around to look at Ella's and Riley's reactions where they're sitting in the back.

"You didn't do anything to me," Ella Quinn says to my dad, mercifully taking the Just Ella thing in stride.

"Exactly," he says. "We didn't listen to Hazel, and that meant that something we could have helped stop went on for longer than it should have. So just like we said sorry to Hazel for not listening to her, we're sorry that we didn't help you when we could have."

One of my parents' books is called *My Bad: How Apologizing to Your Children Can Make You the Cool Parent*. I couldn't bring myself to read that one, but it seems like my dad actually learned something good from it.

"Thanks," Ella Quinn says quietly. If this were last month, I'd assume that small voice meant that she thought my dad was embarrassing, and that I was embarrassing as a result. But now I know it means she means what she's saying. That she's grateful, but a little shy to express it fully. Now it makes me smile.

"You *did* mess up, though," I say. "Just so you know. I'll be milking that for a while."

"We completely messed up," my dad agrees.

"You thought that I was on my *period* when I tried to explain," I remind him. Normally I'd probably freak out a little about saying the phrase *on my period* around my dad, but I think he's more embarrassed than I am.

"To be fair, that was your mom's theory and I didn't have the knowledge or experience to dispute it."

"Point taken." I nod.

"The next time you and your friends single-handedly take

down a culture of harassment and bullying at your school, I promise your mom and I will believe you."

"Okay, but can that wait?" Riley interrupts. "I'm going to need at *least* a year of rest between this takedown and the next, if possible."

When the host of the Chinese restaurant my mom and I go to says *table for seven, one high chair?* my parents shake their heads.

"Actually, could we split that up?" my mom asks, and then turns to Riley, Ella, and me. "You three have earned your own private table."

My mom gives me one last squeeze, and then sits down with my dad, Rowan, and Ella's and Riley's moms at a little table in the corner. The man leads Ella, Riley, and me to a table on the other side of the restaurant, and it's like we're adults all of a sudden— like we could come in here and do this and it wouldn't even be a novelty, like we'd complain about work or boyfriends or something here.

(Not that I'll be complaining about boyfriends, but you get it. I'm a good listener.)

As soon as we sit down, Riley starts going over everything I said during my speech. I appreciate that, because it turns out that when you do something that makes your heart pound in your ears, you don't remember too much of it.

"You were *amazing*," Riley says, and I feel my ears heat up a little. "It was like something out of a *movie!* And then at the end when you looked right at Gates! *Please believe us.* You're a badass."

Ella's been quiet since my dad apologized to her in the car, but she speaks up now.

"Seriously, Hazel. Thank you. I've never seen anything like that before."

"So you're not mad?" I wince.

That had been my one fear. That something even worse would happen to Ella. That Tyler's mom would still see her as *the ringleader* and try to punish her even more. It doesn't look like that's going to happen, at least, but I couldn't be sure that Ella Quinn wouldn't be mad at me for telling the whole school what had been happening.

"Are you *kidding?* That was the coolest thing anyone's ever done for me! No, that was the coolest thing anyone's ever done, ever."

"Jeez, it's like that time I went ziplining with you means *nothing*," Riley says. I nudge her leg with my foot under the table and we both laugh.

The waiter comes to take our orders, and it feels like this could be a real thing. Like we could have more lunches. Like we can be friends without having to fight other people, like we can just relax and hang out. Like Ella will still want to be my friend whether I'm helping her in the same way I was before or not.

Ella excuses herself and goes to the bathroom so it's just me and Riley. She's tracing the zodiac drawing on her menu with one finger and won't look up at me.

"So I wanted to say something," she finally says. "Do you remember when all of this started, how Ella told Tyler she liked girls to get him to leave her alone?"

"Yeah." I laugh. It's funny now, honestly. "And then she told him she had a *crush* on me. Could you *imagine?*"

Ella Quinn is one of my best friends, but that's definitely all she'll ever be.

"I can't picture Ella having a crush on *anyone* for a while after all that," Riley says, and we both laugh. "But I just wanted to say, uh . . . you can trust her, y'know?"

I blush. "What do you mean?"

I can't believe this. Did Ella Quinn tell Riley about me? Everything in my gut sinks to my feet.

"Just that if you ever had something you wanted to tell her, you could," Riley says. She hasn't noticed how freaked out I look. "Or me, obviously. I'm just saying, Ella wouldn't tell anyone."

Ella *did* tell Riley I'm gay. I knew as soon as I started middle school and realized that everyone was having crushes on everyone else that I wasn't going to be the same. I knew that I wasn't going to have best friends, or friends at all, really, and I convinced myself that I was okay with that. I should have just stopped there. I could have helped Ella Quinn without becoming her friend. I shouldn't have gotten so invested. Once you're invested, you can be disappointed. And, since now I'm trying very hard not to cry, I think it's safe to say I'm disappointed.

"I guess I can't trust her that much," I say. "If she told you what I told her."

Riley starts waving her hands, her eyes wide.

"No! She didn't tell me anything. I just wanted to tell you that and say that if there *was* anything, you can trust her not to tell anyone anything. I just . . . thought you might have something you might tell me—I mean, her. I don't know. I just had a feeling. Ella's cool. I know. Seriously."

It takes me a second to figure out what Riley's trying to say, but when I figure it out my eyes bulge out and I get that feeling I had from the other night, when Riley texted me to say my speech was her favorite and I had to stuff my head under a pillow, except now there aren't any pillows so I think I just look like someone's sticking their fingers in my mouth and stretching it because my smile is really, really big. It's embarrassing but I also can't stop, so I think I just have to lean into it.

"Oh!" I say. "You . . . *know?* Like . . . you know the way that I know?"

Riley smiles. She taps my foot with hers under the table. "I know the way you know, y'know?"

We both laugh so hard that we're still laughing when Ella comes back. She gives us a look and says *I'm not even gonna ask.*

"So, did Gates tell you about . . . everything?" I ask Ella Quinn once she sits back down.

"What, about how even after all of that, Tyler might still totally get away with it?"

"That's the one."

Ella Quinn takes a really, really deep breath.

"I mean, obviously we're gonna do it," she says. "Of course we're gonna do the whole thing where we fight tooth and nail to make sure Tyler actually gets punished. But it's gonna take ages, and right now I don't think I want to think about it. We're more interesting than that. So, for today, can we not talk about him?"

I try to hide a smile. I wasn't sure if Ella was going to be willing to put herself on the line again, but there it is. *Obviously we're gonna do it.* Because that's the kind of person she is. The kind of person I'm proud to be friends with.

"We can talk about whatever you want," Riley says. She must be reading my mind again, because she looks over at me and smiles knowingly.

Ella launches into a story about a book she started reading and I let her voice wash over me. It's comfortable, now, to sit with her and Riley and laugh together, to make jokes about each other and know that it's never meant in a mean way. It feels good to be comfortable with people. I smile without thinking and Ella and Riley smile back.

Over the summer, the only reason I was excited to go back to school was because of the speech contest. I thought seventh grade was going to be my year, that I was finally going to win and it didn't matter what else happened, as long as I got that win. I thought it would make me feel better—like it would be worth it to be Quiet Hazel who didn't have any friends as long as I could pretend like I was better than everybody else. Now, Riley rips the tip of her straw wrapper off and tries to blow it at Ella's face.

It doesn't work at *all,* and the three of us laugh so loudly at how upset Riley looks that my mom balls up a napkin and pretends to throw it at us as a warning. It just makes all of us laugh harder, though we try to muffle it in our hands.

I don't even know who won the speech contest this year, and, as I realize that, I also realize that I don't care. I hope they're happy with their win. I would so much rather be here than alone with my first-place ribbon.

Plus, now I have a full year to get ready for the next speech contest.

I make a mental note to write down a few brilliant speech ideas when I get home—I can always kick Ella's butt next year.

AUTHOR'S NOTE

One day, when I was in the sixth grade, I went to the principal's office.

Earlier, two boys were bugging my friends and me during art class. When the teacher wasn't listening, they felt like they could say and do whatever they wanted. They objectified and insulted me. And then, when my friend stood up, one of the boys slapped her on the butt. I told him that was sexual harassment, and he looked me in the eye and said *what are you going to do, tell the principal?*

He really, really didn't think I would do it. He thought he could get away with it. So, I got up, went to the office, and told the principal.

He got suspended for three days, and we all moved on. But when I started to write this note, I messaged that friend to ask if it was okay to tell that story. And she said *that's funny, I was just thinking about that the other day.*

When something like that happens to you, you remember it. I remember all of the boys who saw me as a body, not a person. I remember the ones who used me the way Tyler uses Hazel. Even though it's been years, and I'm a grownup with my own life now, what they did still matters.

I so hope that you don't relate to this book. I hope that you read it and enjoy it, but you walk away from it without it reminding you of anything that's ever happened in your own life. Unfortunately, all those statistics Hazel brings up in her speech are true, which means it's pretty likely that you might find something here that you relate to. Maybe you told someone and the person responsible was punished, the way the boys who harassed my friends and me were. Maybe you told someone and, like with Hazel, Ella, and Riley, they didn't believe you. Or maybe you haven't told anyone, like Maya. Maybe you aren't sure if anyone would ever believe you, or you're afraid of getting in trouble.

The harassment made me angry when it happened. I didn't understand why I was expected to grin and bear it, so I didn't. But not everyone has the same reaction, and not everyone is ready, safe, or empowered to share their stories. But there's one positive—you aren't alone. If you can't talk to an adult, you can talk to a friend. You don't have to make it this massive Very Special Episode of a TV Show No One Really Watches. You can turn to your friend and say *god, that was a messed-up thing to do, wasn't it?*

Thankfully, people are starting to understand that sexual harassment isn't an adults-only issue. If you recognized your own life in Hazel's story, remember that you have options. The organization Stop Sexual Assault in Schools (stopsexualassaultinschools .org) can direct you to resources for yourself and your school. If you want to talk to someone, you can call RAINN at 1-800-656-HOPE or chat with them online.

The more we talk about it, the easier it gets. It's true that sometimes people don't believe you, and it's true that sometimes people believe you and you still don't get the result you deserve. But you don't know what might happen until you try, right?

✳ ACKNOWLEDGMENTS ✳

This book was written on a complete whim—an experiment, to see how it would feel to dive back into the swirling mess that was my head when I was Hazel's age. Turns out that writing all of that down led to the best, most positive experiences I've had so far in my career, and I have a lot of people to thank for that.

First, thank you to my incredible agent, Claire Friedman. I've read a lot of acknowledgments where authors say they have the best agent ever, but I think they must all be lying, because Claire's *the* best. Thank you also to Hannah Schofield for being one of Hazel's earliest and biggest fans, and fighting for her whenever you could.

To Lily Kessinger, my wonderful, thoughtful, funny, kind editor at Clarion. Thank you for seeing Hazel the way she deserves to be seen, and guiding both of us to be our absolute best.

To the rest of the team at Clarion—Emilia Rhodes, Marcie Lawrence, Samira Iravani, and Mary Magrisso—thank you for guiding this project forward and helping bring Hazel into the world. Thank you to Megan Gendell for saving me the embarrassment of publishing a book in which Hazel, Ella Quinn, and Riley attend a "pubic skate." Thank you to Luna Valentine for your absolutely perfect depiction of Hazel.

To my wife, Gabi: when I saw my life stretching out long and dark and foggy in front of me, I never even let myself think I'd have someone like you beside me for it. Thank you for the life we've built and for everything to come.

Thank you to Rebecca Barrow for being the best mentor and best best friend I've ever had. Thank you to Rory Power for listening to every crazy thought I've ever had and just being like *yeah, same.* Thank you to both of you for keeping me together.

Thank you to Chelsea Bould and Orla Kinsella for being my earliest readers and biggest fans. Thank you to Emily Downey and Emma Oerton for permission to use your stories in my author's note. Thank you to Sama Abdi for living through 2019 with me.

I've been a Writing Person since I was barely older than Hazel, and I've been able to know so many wonderful people as a result of that. Thank you to Paige Cober, Sierra Elmore, Hannah Whitten, Marisa Kanter, Grace Li, Meryl Wilsner, Kelsey Rodkey, Jake Arlow, Keely Weiss, Claribel Ortega, Kiki Nguyen, Kate Cochrane, and *so many* other people who've been around for the last decade-plus. Thank you to Jess Wragg, Nadine Collins, Rosie Murphy, Jaimie Poyner, and Emma Grønning for helping me survive uni.

Thank you to my family—to my mom, for going easy on me when I almost failed tenth-grade science because I'd been doing NaNoWriMo, and to my brother, Mitchell, for thinking what I do is actually cool. Thank you to my dad, for knowing me so perfectly. I miss you every day. Thank you to Alex Buckingham for being a ridiculously perfect mother-in-law and G-ma. Thank you to Cam Roylance, my grandfather, and thank you to Cam Roylance, my cousin. Thank you to Heather Adolphe for every drink you've ever poured me.

Hazel deals with a lot of teachers, good and bad, but I'd like to thank a few of my good ones. Mrs. Parsons, Mr. Parker, Ms. Butler, Ms. Valentine, Ms. Cushman, Mrs. Wright, Mr. Innocenzi, Leander Reeves, Sarah Franklin, Jane Potter, Beverly Tarquini: thank you. Special thanks to Mr. Butcher, who once refused to answer a question I asked because I had used the word *gonna*, thus spurring me on to publish a book with *Gonna* in the title. Your move, Butcher.

Finally, thank you to anyone who's ever stood up for themselves, for others, or for what they believe in. Me and Hazel are so proud of you.